Playing for Keeps

Stephanie Morris

Amira Press, LLC

Playing for Keeps
Stephanie Morris

ISBN: 978-1-935348-75-7

Publisher:
Amira Press, LLC
Baltimore, MD
www.amirapress.com

Dedication

To my Dad, my guardian angel in the sky.
I will always be daddy's little girl.
To my Grandma Madea for all of her
unconditional love and support over the years.

Chapter One

"Hi, Mr. Feldon."

Her former high school principal grinned and stepped back, allowing her to enter his home. "Hello, Keirra. Come on in."

She stepped inside with relief. Today had been a busy day. She had spent it running errands and dodging Eric. He had been trailing her all day for some reason. Hopefully neither of her big-mouth sisters had made mention of her flippant remark about Eric last night. Of course, she had just wanted to tease her sisters, and because of it, this morning at the breakfast table had been so funny. Her sisters had almost given her a full-body inspection. Luckily, she had gone downstairs dressed for work instead of her normal pajamas, so there wasn't much they could examine. It served them right. The only thing now was that she had to deal with Eric.

Thankfully, she hadn't had too much contact with Eric since the homecoming celebration. She had only run into him once, and she had been getting in her car so she had been able to get away quickly. Deep down, she knew she wasn't going to be so fortunate today. She had thought he was going to be able to catch her in the grocery store while she was picking up Mr. Feldon's groceries, but she had been a little quicker than him. She had to stay away from Eric. Something about the man scared her to death. He made her weak in ways that she didn't want to be.

"Keirra, are you going to bring the groceries in here?"

Keirra jumped at the sound of her name, and then began to flush in embarrassment. She was still standing in the foyer like a brainless person. Smiling, she gave him an apologetic look. "Sorry, Mr. Feldon. I fell asleep for a minute there."

Mr. Feldon chuckled and gave her a knowing look. "Is that what they call it now?"

Keirra couldn't help but to laugh as she followed Mr. Feldon into the kitchen. She winced when she realized how nervous and high-pitched it sounded. Mr. Feldon was an astute man, and he would figure out that something was amiss and soon, if she wasn't careful.

"How are you feeling?"

He nodded. "I am feeling a lot better. My son will be in town within the next month or so."

Keirra smiled. "That's good."

"Actually it's great. I will be able to get rid of the nurse from hell."

Keirra laughed before she could stop herself. "Mr. Feldon, that isn't nice."

He chuckled. "That may be the case, but it's true."

Keirra just shook her head and began to unpack the grocery bags. It didn't take her as long as she would have liked it to. She was glad Mr. Feldon invited her to stay and visit. He led her to the living room, and she sat down on the sofa while he sat down across from her in the recliner.

"So who is the young man that has you running scared?"

Keirra's eyes widened, but she couldn't deny anything, and even if she tried, Mr. Feldon wouldn't have believed it.

"Is he the one waiting for you outside of my home?"

Keirra fell for the ploy and turned around to look out the window. Once she realized the blinds were closed she knew she'd been had. Still, she was positive that Eric was out there waiting on her.

"I was wondering why you were beating on my door like you had a murderer on your heels."

Keirra dropped her head and thought she was going to die of embarrassment.

"So do I need to invite the young man in?"

Keirra stood up quickly shaking her head. It was the last thing she needed, another person to get in her business. He would only become another ally of Eric's and try to persuade her to go out with him. She stood quickly picking up her purse and smiled at Mr. Feldon.

"No that's okay, Mr. Feldon. I will go out and talk to him. It was nice seeing and talking to you. Glad to see that you are feeling better." She said the words so quickly she was certain she set a record and rushed for the door, setting another. Mr. Feldon had barely stood up, and Keirra had let herself out the door. It was already closing behind her. He chuckled when he heard her stomp her foot.

"Damn it," Keirra muttered as she laid eyes on Eric. Even though she knew he had still been out there, seeing him made it a little worse. She looked up as the door swung open.

"I heard that, young lady."

Keirra stumbled over an apology. She wasn't sorry for saying the curse word but for letting Mr. Feldon hear her say it. The events of the past ten minutes made her want to crawl underground and hide. Unfortunately, she wouldn't fit. Even if she did, she wouldn't be able to burrow quickly enough. Taking a deep breath, she walked down the driveway toward Eric. His mysterious expression didn't change as she made her way toward him. As she got closer to him, the first thing she noticed was he smelled delicious. The second thing was he was sexy as hell. She stopped in front of him, and he spoke before she could.

"I will meet you at Sam's Café in ten minutes. We definitely need to talk."

Before she could say anything, he turned and climbed into his SUV before driving off. She stood there for a moment flabbergasted at his actions. After another moment, she went and climbed into her car. As she backed out of the driveway, she could have sworn she saw a laughing Mr. Feldon glancing out of the window. She blinked, and when she refocused her eyes, no one was there.

Something was definitely wrong with her. Her avoidance of Eric was starting to drive her insane. She continued to back out of the driveway. When she made it to the stop sign, she started to turn in the direction of her house. It would serve Eric right, yet she knew he would come looking for her, and once he found her, there would be no telling what he would do. She would rather meet him on neutral ground. This way no one had the upper hand, although he already had a slight one by inviting her to Sam's Café the way that he had.

No. She wasn't going to back down, but then she was curious to see what he had to say. Knowing the turn she was going to make was sure to lead to trouble, she still took it. When she pulled up, Eric was already there. Keirra took a deep breath before getting out of her car. She walked into Sam's Café and spotted Eric at the back of the restaurant. One of the things that she noticed was that he stood out. He had a commanding presence.

What she did know was that whatever he had to say better be interesting because she was going to have a fit otherwise. As she neared him, she figured whatever he had to say must be important because he was sitting in a secluded booth. He stood up as she approached the booth and didn't sit back down until she was seated. She hated that he was such a gentleman. Personally, she thought it was all an act to sucker a woman in, and she refused to be one of the women that fell for that game. So much so that she didn't even give him a chance to speak.

"So what did you want to talk about?"

If she had irritated him by interrupting him, he didn't let it show. Instead, he gave her a reassuring smile.

"Why don't we order some food first then we can talk."

She frowned at him. "I'm not hungry."

"You have to be. You haven't eaten all day."

Keirra laughed. "So you admit that you have been following me all day?"

Eric grinned. "I wasn't aware that I was trying to make it a secret."

Keirra figured he had a point. If he wanted to trail her without her knowing, his experience as an officer would allow him to do so.

"Well, thank you for the offer of lunch, but I had a big breakfast."

As if to mock her as well as make her look like a liar, her stomach let out a loud growl. She closed her eyes in embarrassment and wondered if the day could get any worse. Eric chuckled and leaned back in the booth.

"Are you sure?"

Keirra rolled her eyes at his smugness before picking up the menu in defeat. She flipped through the menu in haste and decided on the chicken fried steak sandwich. That was one of the things on the menu she had been interested in trying but hadn't received the chance to. Eric must have worked up an appetite following her around because he ordered enough food to feed at least three people. There was no way the man could eat the way he did and maintain the body he had. The shock must have shown on her face because he smiled.

"Don't worry. I have a workout room at my house, so I get plenty of exercise, but you are always welcome to provide alternative methods."

Keirra gasped in outrage, but she didn't get the chance to respond because Nadia came up to their table and took their drink and food orders. When Nadia walked off, Keirra turned her attention back to Eric.

"So what was so important that I had to meet you here and have lunch?" she asked through gritted teeth, still insulted by his earlier comment. However, she wasn't going to give him the satisfaction of a response. He would only bait her into an argument, and frankly, she just didn't want to go there.

Eric laughed, and her heart skipped a few beats. The man was too sexy for his own good.

"To discuss that you want me just as much as I want you, and it's time we stop avoiding it."

Keirra felt her eyes widen. The man was cocky as well. A little too cocky, and it made her blood pressure rise to a dangerous point.

"I tell you what. When you are ready to talk to me and not at me, let me know."

Keirra reached for her purse and went to slide out of the booth. Eric reached out and stopped her.

"Keirra, wait. I apologize if I sounded rude."

Keirra gave him an incredulous look. "*If you sounded rude?*"

She took a deep breath and tried to calm her nerves before continuing. "Eric, you were *very rude,* and you know it. What I can also tell you is that I'm not like the other women you have talked to. So you are going to have to do much better than this if you want to capture my attention."

Keirra tightened her grip on her purse at the thought of just how many women that could be. "If you are looking for a typical one, I am positive there are several women around here willing to oblige you starting with Melanie."

Eric gave her an incredulous look, but she wasn't going to take the words back. If he wanted a battle, he was going to get one.

* * * *

Eric stared at the enigma of a woman sitting across from him and thought about the bold statement she'd just made. He completely ignored the examples of rudeness she had displayed toward him because he could easily point them out, but they wouldn't help him any. "I don't want any other woman. I want you."

The smile that appeared on her face wasn't one of humor. "And I am sure you're one who always gets what he wants."

Eric shrugged his shoulders. "I won't say always, but I do a lot of the time." Keirra just shook her head. "Well, that could be your problem."

Eric shook his head. "There isn't anything wrong with getting what you want."

"It is if it turns you into a spoiled pompous ass."

Eric tilted his head to the side. "Do you really think that I am spoiled?" Keirra laughed. "I know you are."

Eric was quiet for a moment, a lot longer than he wanted to be, because Nadia appeared at the table with their drinks. When she walked off again, Eric spoke.

"I think I deserve a chance to prove to you that I'm not the bad man you think I am."

He groaned inwardly at the expression that appeared on her face. Inadvertently, he just gave her an opening, and she looked happy to use it.

"First off, I never said that you were a bad man. Second of all, if you are a good and honorable man, then you will let me come to that conclusion on my own."

Eric frowned because he knew where Keirra was going with her reasoning. "And how long will it take for you to come to your conclusion?"

Keirra smiled. "That is where your patience is going to have to come in. For you see, Mr. Brooks, you can't rush these sorts of things."

Eric closed his eyes and sat back in the booth. He knew he had just been beaten at his own game. The only thing Keirra didn't know was he wanted her more than his next breath, and he intended to seduce her until her every waking thought was about him.

Chapter Two

Eric leaned back in his chair and propped his feet up on his desk. He was tired, but he hadn't done anything except stay up all night and think about Keirra. He just wanted to find a good woman to settle down with. Keirra was that woman. When he had run into her yesterday, she had looked as beautiful as she always looked. Every time he saw her, he couldn't take his eyes off her for more than a few minutes. The only thing he didn't like was he was beginning to think about Keirra a little more than he should. He didn't know what his problem was. He couldn't figure out what it was about her that made him look at her in a way he hadn't looked at any other woman. He wouldn't mind using other tactics to get Keirra to go out with him. A man would have to be a fool to turn down an opportunity with a beautiful woman.

Her expressive brown eyes always made him wonder what she was thinking. Was she undressing him with her eyes or cursing him? Keirra knew he was interested in her. But she fought it. In his opinion, she just wanted to ignore the attraction between the two of them. He didn't know why he was wasting so much time on Keirra because he didn't have trouble attracting a woman. It was obvious that Keirra didn't want to date him. Yet, it didn't diminish his attraction to her. If anything, it only made his attraction to her stronger. He was used to women fawning all over him, and it was a little refreshing not to have one who did.

"Eric, can I see you in my office for a minute?"

Eric groaned. He had just gotten comfortable. He swung his feet onto the floor, then stood up and walked into Randy's office. He liked working with Randy. Eric hadn't been certain what made him apply for the deputy position, but he had. It had been a good move and a relief from the burnout he had started to feel after spending ten years on the Atlanta police force. Randy was the Appling County sheriff, and he was a good sheriff.

"Have a seat and wipe that look off your face. I'm not putting you to work."

Eric chuckled and took a seat. "Thanks I think."

Randy shook his head and leaned back into his chair. "I just called you in the office to be nosey and see how things were going with Keirra."

Eric sighed. "Seems to be going downhill since the dance."

It was true. Keirra had begun to warm up to him, and now he was right back to where he started. She had something against cops, and he was going to find out what it was. He knew from a background check that she hadn't had any run-ins with the law, but there was something feeding her dislike.

"I will get it figured out."

Randy smiled. "I am sure you will. Just keep in mind she is a good woman, and she is more fragile than she looks."

Eric wondered what Randy meant but didn't ask. He had a feeling it would just lead to more questions, and he had enough of those as it was. Instead he sighed and stood up. "Now that much I knew. If you have any more advice, I would appreciate it."

Randy nodded at Eric. Eric left Randy's office. He knew he had his work cut out for him. His playboy past had gotten him into deep trouble at times, but those days were over. He wasn't sure if turning thirty-two, meeting Keirra, seeing all of his friends and sisters get married, or a combination of all the events were influencing him to want to settle down. Then again it could be all the slaps upside his head from his mom and sisters when he'd done something stupid in the past. Either way he was ready to settle down and preferably with Keirra.

He walked back to his desk and retook his seat. When Gary made it back it would be his turn to patrol, and that was more than okay with him. Sometimes he missed the fast pace in Atlanta, and sometimes he didn't.

He didn't know how many ulcers he had during his ten years on the force. There were some pretty scars to show for it too. Mainly scuffle wounds, a knife wound on his left arm, and a scar from where a bullet grazed him on his right arm. The knife wound had been the scariest. Wrestling a knife from a drug addict on speed was a task he never wanted to face again. The guy seemed to be invincible when it came to pain. It had taken the assistance of three other officers to get the guys under control, although they had all suffered bruises, scrapes, and cuts.

He looked up as the door opened, and Gary walked in. Eric stood up and gathered his keys and hat. He liked the hat. It shaded his eyes against the sun, and now that it was starting to get cold, the hat kept his head warm.

"Pretty slow today."

Eric smiled. "No slower than it is in here."

Gary chuckled. "You have a point there."

"Well I need some fresh air, so I'm going on patrol."

Gary sat down at his desk. "See you when you get back.

Eric turned and walked out of the station, his mind still on Keirra and the conversation he just had with Randy. Despite his disastrous lunch with her he planned to pursue her. She was different from the women he had dated in the past. He was used to dating women who didn't want a long-term relationship. If they were with him they knew he felt the same, and nothing would come of the relationship except pure satisfaction. Even so, some of the women would forget the rules and become clingy, and he would have to call the casual relationship to an end.

His job as a cop in Atlanta had made it difficult to date anyone on a serious level. Before he left Atlanta, he had vowed no more women with emotional hang-ups about what he did for a living.

However, he had had no idea he would meet Keirra. His rule was changing, and he didn't mind. Keirra was a dynamic woman, and different from the women he had dated in the past. They suited each other well, and there were things about her that reminded him of everything he could want in a woman.

Getting in his car he had one place in mind to patrol. He maneuvered through the town to the Smith's residence with ease. Driving by the house he smiled. It must be his lucky day. Keirra's car was the in the driveway, and she was standing outside washing it. He pulled over to the curb and stepped out of his car.

When he closed the door Keirra turned around, and he felt like he had been punched in the stomach at her beauty. She was in a tank top, exposing smooth skin and a toned body. Cotton shorts revealed long legs that should never be covered up by the jeans and pants she always wore. He smiled at the curse word that came out of her mouth and started up the driveway.

"I didn't know you knew those kinds of words."

She opened her mouth to respond, but he cut her off. "I wonder if you talk to all people like this, or if is it only reserved for me."

Her heated look could have melted metal. "It depends," she growled.

"On what?"

She crossed her arms and took a defensive stance. "On whether you are here to talk to me."

He smiled and stepped closer to her, taking slight satisfaction when she took a step back before catching herself. He affected her more than she let on.

"Well, of course I am here to talk to you."

His smile widened when he heard her groan and drop her head. Then he watched her shoulders stiffen as if she were preparing for a battle with him. If she wanted a battle she would get one.

"Then yes, the curse word was for you. How can I help you, deputy?" she asked, and went back to washing her car. If she thought she could dismiss him by presenting him with her back she had a lot to learn about him.

"You know I could charge you with verbal assault of a public servant."

His statement made her stop in mid-scrub, and he watched her shoulders stiffen even more as if it were possible. When she turned to look at him, he knew exactly what Randy had meant earlier. If he had been a lesser man he would have shrank back from her angry gaze.

"I don't play those kinds of games, Deputy Brooks."

He knew he needed to back off, but he couldn't force himself to. *"Challenge her."* Kristen's words of wisdom back at the dance after homecoming rang out in his ears. *"She enjoys being challenged."*

Her eyes were spitting fire, but despite her anger, Keirra was exquisite to him, and his interest in her deepened. He had to find a way to get through to her.

"You know all of this could go away if you would just take me up on my peace offer. How about dinner Friday night?"

Keirra placed the towel she was using back in the bucket before turning to face him, yet her eyes were ablaze in them.

"Now *that*, deputy, sounds like an illegal solicitation of a citizen, not to mention bribery. I wonder how many charges I could press against you."

He had to laugh. She had a lot of stubbornness and had risen to the challenge. She was also tough. If he ever had another witness he needed to interrogate he would use her to play the bad cop.

"Now for the last time, deputy, I'm not, and will never be, interested in any offering you are trying to make."

He held up his hands in surrender, and some of the anger in her eyes died down, but not enough for him to drop his guard.

"Do you mind if I ask why?"

The fire sparked back up, and her teeth clenched. "I don't like cops."

Eric wanted to ask more questions because he felt like they were getting somewhere, but he knew he had pushed his limit for the day, so instead he tipped his hat in her direction.

"I will go for now, Keirra, but know this conversation isn't finished. Not by a long shot."

She glared at him. "For your sake, I hope it is. Have a pleasant day, Deputy Brooks."

He smiled wondering how she could get so much venom in her voice. He wanted to know if there was ever a time when the rancor wasn't there. Opening the door to his patrol car, he stopped and turned to look back at Keirra. He didn't know right now, but he planned to find out.

* * * *

"Kayla."

"I am in the kitchen."

Keirra followed her sister's voice into the kitchen and found her pulling out leftovers from the refrigerator. She went over and began to help. "It is a little different not having Kristen around, huh?"

Kayla groaned. "Don't remind me."

This was the first time that she and her sisters didn't live together, and it was very different. Then again so was being a triplet. She and her sisters had done just about everything in life together. Now Kristen had fallen in love with Randy again and had moved out of the house. Keirra was certain that wedding bells would be ringing soon. Kristen and Randy had a history that couldn't be denied.

She smiled when she thought about the antics her sister had come up with to avoid Randy when they had first moved back to Baxley. She had used a few of them herself to avoid Eric.

Kristen had written all of her plans down on a tablet and had tried to put the plan into action, but the day Randy enrolled Wade into Kristen's daycare, the plan had gone awry, and Kristen had given into her leftover feelings for Randy. Keirra was happy her sister had found the man for her. Keirra popped a container into the microwave and grinned at Kayla.

"We knew it would happen sooner or later."

Kayla nodded. "True, but it still feels different."

Keirra leaned against the counter. "So which one of us do you think will be bitten by the love bug next?"

Kayla laughed. "As if you have to ask."

Keirra shook her head. There was no way she was going to fall in love with Eric Brooks.

"My money is on you."

"Well, it is a good thing I'm not going to bet against you because, little sister, you would be broke."

Keirra laughed, pulled the first container out of the microwave, and slipped another inside. She loved her sisters.

"So did you see Deputy Brooks today?"

Keirra groaned. Lately she had seen the man every day, which was just a little too much for her. "Don't start, Kayla."

Kayla just shook her head. "Well, if you ask me, I say that you are insane. The man is intelligent, he had a job, he looks good, and he follows the law."

Keirra gave her a teasing look. "Well imagine that. You know he's a deputy right?"

Keirra couldn't stop the contempt that came into her voice when she said the word *deputy*.

It was Kayla's turn to groan. "Not again. How come you can't leave that in the past?"

Keirra flinched as if she had been physically struck. "How can you say that, Kayla? He was our *father.*"

Keirra couldn't forget the past even if she wanted to. Kayla came over to her and put an arm around her. "Now you know what I meant. You know as well as I do I could never forget Dad, but I doubt he would want you to spend your life disliking officers of the law because of possible outcomes of having the job."

Keirra held up her hands. "I never said I didn't like cops. I just don't date them."

Kayla laughed and placed an arm around her sister's shoulders, but Keirra didn't find it comforting in the least. She did everything to avoid cops period, including driving at least one mile per hour below the posted speed limit. She never broke any laws. Neither had her sisters, but it was out of habit, and their parents had raised them to be good people. She also wanted to stay as far away from officers as possible. The sight of their uniforms always stirred up bad memories for her.

She could admit that she'd taken her obsession to the extreme, but it was worth it. Their mother had worried herself sick over Keirra after her father had been shot and killed in the line of duty. Now she saw how it was possible, and she refused to do it to herself. She would back off before she let it happen. It was amazing to her how the traumatic experience had affected the three of them differently.

"Take advantage of the situation. Not many women have good men chasing after them."

She listened as Kayla tried to convince her it was unlikely that a shootout like the one that occurred in Atlanta would happen in Baxley. Sure there was always a chance he could be injured. Then again, so could she. She wanted to scream at her for trying to be so rational.

But more importantly Kayla had a point. There was no reason why she couldn't get to know Eric. The worse that could happen was that they might found out that they weren't meant for each other. If he broke her heart, she would deal with it. Kristen had been able to deal with hers, and from a man that she truly loved, so she should be able to do it. Especially since she didn't plan on falling in love with Eric.

This could benefit the both of them. He was an attractive man, a very attractive man. Every time she saw him, his soulful chocolate eyes and untamed curly dark hair gave him an exotic look making her question his parentage. Even as she thought about his hair she to had to restrain from reaching out to touch it. Every since she had seen him she had thought about touching his hair. Maybe she would get the chance to do that now. Eric was deliciously sexy, and that was a plus. Yet, she wanted to know that there was more. She sighed and looked over at her sister.

"What do I have to do to prove to you I don't have anything against Eric being an officer?"

As soon as the words were out of her mouth, she regretted them. It was too late to take the words back. Kayla let go of her and walked over to the cordless phone. She took it off the base and walked back over to Keirra and handed the phone to her.

Kayla smiled. "Call him and ask him on a date."

Keirra almost recoiled, but she couldn't go back and change what she had said. Then she smiled at the loophole that she had just remembered. "I don't have his number."

"Randy does."

Keirra's grin disappeared, and she took the phone out of her sister's hands. It was more of a snatching motion, and she tried to calm her nerves. To be truthful she was starting to think her resistance to Eric was because he was Eric and not because he was an officer of the law. It had gotten to the point where she was forgetting that he was.

The only time she seemed to remember was when she saw him in uniform or when someone made mention of it. She was doing her best to resist Eric's charm and good looks. Taking one last deep breath, she dialed the number to Kristen's cell phone instead of Randy's house phone. She was going to try to make this as easy on herself as possible. After eight hours with her seventh- and eighth-grade students, she couldn't manage to complete any more difficult tasks than that one.

Kristen answered on the second ring. "Hello."

"Hi, Kristen."

She could hear the smile in her sister's voice. "Hey, Keirra. What is going on?"

Keirra paused too long, and Kayla poked her. "I was wondering if you have Eric's number."

It was Kristen's turn to pause now. "Why?"

Keirra cleared her throat before muttering. "I want to ask Eric out on a date."

Kristen's sharp crack of laughter traveled across the line, and Keirra pulled the phone away from her ear to save the rest of her hearing. Once the laughter died down, she placed the phone back to her ear.

"What bet have you and Kayla made this time?"

Kristen could barely get the words out without laughing. Keirra closed her eyes. She had no idea why she thought Kristen might take pity on her. That must have been asking for too much. She tried to work her way out of her sister's humor. "What makes you think there was a bet? I could have decided to do this on my own."

Kristen still sounded as though she were struggling to hold back her laughter. "That's just it. You could have, but you wouldn't."

Keirra sighed. She wasn't so bad, but once she stopped to think about it, she realized she was, and it was embarrassing.

"Do you have his number or not?"

Kristen fell into another round of laughter, and this time Kayla joined her. Keirra ignored both of them, knowing that Kayla's time was coming and that she would find another way to torture Kristen.

Kayla placed the memo board that hung on the fridge in Keirra's hands. A second later, Kristen found the number and relayed it to her.

"Thanks."

She hung up the phone before Kristen could come up with any more snide remarks. She was sure she would pay for it later, but it would be worth it. Kayla was going to bother her enough to the point where she didn't care. She quickly dialed Eric's number into the phone and pressed the talk button. The phone dialed, and she became a little upset when the phone rang four times before he answered it. She didn't pause once he did.

"Hello, Eric, this is Kristen. Would you like to come over for dinner this Friday night?"

She could feel his surprise more than she could hear it. Eric was silent for a long moment.

"Who is this again?"

She heard the smile in voice, and it infuriated her, but if he thought she was going to beg, he had another thing coming. The only thing Kayla had dared her to do was to call Eric and ask him out. She couldn't help it when she growled her name. Unfortunately, she growled a lot of when it came to him. He asked her what she wanted again, and she almost hung up the phone. Instead, she turned her back to Kayla, who was grinning in a sickening fashion before counting to ten silently. After she collected herself, she spoke again.

"I asked if you wanted to come over Friday night for dinner."

She figured that if he came to the house, she would be on her own territory, and therefore, she would feel more secure.

"What time should I be over?"

"Seven is fine," she replied through clenched teeth.

He chuckled. "Do I need to bring anything?"

"Just yourself," she muttered.

"Thank you for inviting me. I am looking forward to it just as much as you are," he stated with slight sarcasm. She refused to be baited.

"You are welcome. Have a good evening."

She hung up the phone, really wishing that she could slam it down. Releasing the breath she had been holding, she walked over to the base and hung it up. She looked over at Kayla who was now dishing leftovers onto two plates.

"It went well, I assume?" Kayla asked innocently.

"As well as can be expected," she replied through clenched teeth.

Kayla smiled. "So what are you going to cook Friday night?"

Keirra groaned and slapped her forehead. In her haste to take the easy way out she had forgotten she would have to cook.

If she didn't cook, he would think that she was too lazy or that she didn't know how. Even though neither assumption would be correct, she didn't want it to appear that way. Then again, why she did care? She wasn't trying to impress him. Frowning, she cursed herself silently. This had been a trap all the way around, and she, being the person who could never walk away from a challenge, had fallen for it. Sitting down at the table to eat her dinner, she began to devise a plan to ensure she came out on top.

Chapter Three

"Kristen, Eric is here."

Eric looked up as Kristen came out of the kitchen. The woman was breathtaking. She was wearing a purple floral-print tube dress and a matching pair of flip-flops. The dress matched her cocoa skin complexion perfectly. Her curly dark brown hair fell a few inches below her shoulder. And the unruly mass was pinned back on the sides with two hair clips.

Realizing it was the first time that he'd seen her with her hair down, he paused. He itched to reach out to touch it, but he resisted. He could only imagine what kind of response it would provoke from her. A smile was pasted onto her face, but he could tell it was strained confirming his suspicion that this invite wasn't completely her idea. Being the competitive person she was, he was certain she'd lost a bet of some sort, and this was the result. Either way, he was going to capitalize on his gain.

"Hello. I am glad that you could join us."

Kayla shook her head. She picked up her purse. "Actually, I have a date myself, so I need to get going."

Eric concealed his grin when Keirra began to look like she was going to spit at the shocking announcement, but she didn't say a word. Instead, he watched as she nodded and followed her sister to the door with a threat of bodily harm through clenched teeth. Kayla just laughed and walked out of the front door. He had to struggle to keep his expression neutral. His night was already going to be eventful enough as it was.

* * * *

Kayla could hardly contain herself. She walked down the driveway before climbing into her car and drove over to Randy and Kristen's place before smiling. She had lied to Keirra once again about having a date or at least a real one. It served her sister right. When she realized Keirra had planned to use her as a safety blanket, she had quickly made her own plans. Eric and Keirra belonged together, and the sooner Keirra realized that, the better it would be.

Kayla pulled into the driveway of the home her sister shared with Randy and parked. Getting out of her car, she walked up the walkway and rang the doorbell. A second later, it swung open, and Kristen and Wade stood there. The little tyke threw himself at her, and Kayla caught him. Even though Randy and Kristen weren't married yet, Kayla still considered Wade to be her nephew.

She greeted her sister as she walked into the house. "Glad you could join us. Wade and I were just getting ready to order pizza."

Kayla placed a kiss on Wade's cheek. "Sounds good."

Kristen closed the door. "Randy should be home shortly."

Kayla laughed. "I promise I won't stay too late. Just long enough to make Keirra sweat a little, although I am contemplating staying for a few hours."

Kristen shook her head. "Don't you feel a little guilty?"

Kayla shook her head. "Not at all. I am helping her out whether she realizes or not."

Still, she knew that there was going to be hell to pay later. Keirra was going to throw an outrageous temper tantrum when she found out what Kayla had done. Yet, it was worth it. Anyone with eyes could see that Eric was a good guy. Keirra deserved a guy that would treat her the way that she deserved and challenge her while doing it. Keirra was always torturing them about something. So it was only fair that she tortured Keirra a little. Something told her it would be worth it.

* * * *

Keirra took a deep breath as she closed the door behind Kayla and turned to face Eric. Her face hurt from the attempt to keep her smile in place. "I hope you are hungry."

Eric grinned. "Starved."

She led the way to the kitchen. He inhaled deeply when they entered the kitchen. "Something smells good."

She heard the sincerity in his voice and accepted his compliment. "Thank you."

She led him to the table where a sirloin tip roast was waiting with a platter or rolls, a dish of green beans and macaroni and cheese next to it. "Have a seat. What would you like to drink?"

"A beer if you have it."

She nodded, went to the refrigerator to grab a beer for him, and picked up the glass of wine that she'd been nursing while she prepared dinner. She set his drink down then took her seat across from him.

"This looks good."

This time when she smiled it didn't feel as forced. "Thank you."

"How did you learn to cook so well?"

She stopped in the process of putting the sirloin steak on his plate. "How do you know that it is good?"

He grinned. "Hey, if it looks good, it is bound to taste good."

Keirra shook her head smiling. Men could be so naive. Yes, it was true her cooking was good, but she had been to places where the food had looked good and tasted awful. When she finished serving him, she served herself.

"If you don't mind, I would like a little more."

She shook her head and handed him the utensils. Her eyes widened as she watched him load the food onto his plate. She looked down at her own plate when she thought back to his offer of her helping him to stay in shape in other ways. Right now, she had to admit she was tempted as he sat across from her.

She cleared her throat and tried to clear her mind of the provocative thoughts before she began to eat. The last thing she wanted was for her food to get cold, although the hot thoughts she was having would probably balance it out.

"This is really good."

Keirra tried not to smile at the heartfelt compliment. She didn't want to encourage him, but the corner of her mouth still tilted up. "Thanks."

They ate in silence for a moment before he reached for his beer. "Tell me something about you that I don't already know."

She paused for moment and tried to think of something he didn't know about her before responding. "I am a virgin."

Eric began to choke, and Keirra resumed eating innocently. He finally pulled himself together. "Excuse me?"

She knew it hadn't been something he had expected to hear from her. She made the statement so he would be out of his element because she was definitely out of hers. Still his expression was comical.

She gave him an innocent shrug. "You said to tell you something you didn't already know."

He gave her a level look. "Well, that wasn't exactly what I was referring to."

She just shrugged. The shock factor had been what she was going for, and it seemed to have worked.

He paused, and she could tell he was choosing his words wisely. "Do you mind tell me why?"

"I haven't found a man that I wanted to share myself with."

* * * *

Eric remained silent. He respected her decision. A woman who valued herself enough to know what she wanted was a woman that he could admire. His mother had also always told him to respect a woman even if she didn't respect herself. He'd had a lot of girlfriends over the years, but he could still count how many women he had been with on one hand and not use up all of his fingers. True, he had the reputation of being a playboy, but he was smart. There was too much going around for him to take the risk even with protection.

She smiled at him. "Tell me something about you that I don't know."

Eric grinned. "I am the youngest of four and the only boy."

Keirra paused in the middle of the bite of food she had been about to take.

"And you are a playboy? Do your sisters know?"

He smiled wickedly. "Yes they do, and I have the permanent knot in the back of my head to prove it."

Her eyebrows rose. "Any of them come from the women you have been involved with?"

He shook his head. "I have never given any of them any reason to."

She scoffed. "A polite playboy?"

His chuckled. "Most are."

"Well, I wouldn't know since I have never been the acquaintance of one until now."

"I will try to make it a memorable experience then."

She resumed eating, and he did as well. Once he had his fill, he pushed his plate away. He had cleaned it. The food had been as good as it looked. The woman could cook.

"Did you save room for dessert?"

He groaned in agony as he shook his head. "No."

She laughed. "Well, it is a good thing that I didn't make any, but we do have some lemon-drop cookies if you do."

He nodded but remained seated and continued to stare at her. The woman was beautiful. She was tall and curvy in every spot that she should be. Her brown eyes were intense and full of desire in his opinion. He was tempted to ask her what she was thinking, but she wouldn't tell him if he did so he wouldn't. He smiled when she gave him a look of irritation and impatience.

"Are you going to stop staring at me?"

He shook his head slowly. "No."

She tilted her head to the side. "It isn't polite to stare."

He laughed. "Oh, so you do know the meaning of the word?"

Her eyes widened at his sharp remark. "You—*oh*!"

She jumped up from the table, knocking her chair over in the process. He knew he caught her off guard when he touched her leg.

Her look became even more irritated. "Why are you touching me?"

He stood and stalked around the table to her, like she was the prey and he was the predator. She backed up as he continued toward her.

"Why not? You didn't seem to mind a few weeks ago."

He didn't stop until her back hit the fridge. There wasn't any fear in her eyes, only anxiety. She licked her lips before she spoke, and he followed the movement with his eyes. "That was different."

He stepped closer to her. "How?"

She shrugged, and he liked that she seemed to be so affected by his nearness. He couldn't ever recall her being speechless around him.

"Are you afraid of me, Keirra, or is it the uniform?"

Her eyes widened as if he hit her conflicts dead-on. He leaned closer to her, and she shrank back before she seemed to catch herself. He watched her stiffen her shoulders.

"Neither."

She tried to step away, but he wouldn't let her. He brought his hands up and bracketed her body in between them.

"I think it may be both."

She shook her head in denial, but he continued speaking. "I think you believe that I am too much of a man for you. That I will get inside your castle you've built and give you a little taste of everything you want before breaking your heart by walking away."

A gasp escaped her, but he kept talking. "I bet that the men that you have dated have been weak minded and didn't give you anywhere near the challenge that you need."

As if it were possible, Eric stepped closer to her.

"I should tell you that I plan to challenge you. Challenge you beyond your wildest dreams."

Instead of giving her time to answer, he stepped even closer to her. He couldn't recall ever wanting a woman so badly. When he stood directly in front of her, he reached out and cupped the back of her neck to guide her mouth to meet his.

The moment their lips touched he felt it. Passion so thick you could cut it. And when he went past her moist lips and inserted his tongue inside her mouth, he knew he had been anticipating this very moment ever since the night they met.

He was surprised when her response was immediate, absolute and totally appetizing. The reason they were here might be incidental, but the sexual chemistry between them was as instantaneous and unprompted as it could get. The depth of her sensuality was enough to make him want to jump into Lake Mayers to cool off. A cold shower just wouldn't work off the heat.

He had discovered ever since he had met her at Sam's Cafe, that he desired her to the point of madness. And this was the result. He was getting a pretty good taste of her, and she was getting a good taste of him, as well.

He heard her groan low in her throat and knew if he pushed hard enough they would be making love right here, possibly on the floor, which wasn't where he wanted their first time to be. The spectacle they would cause would be bail worthy. He knew she could feel how aroused he was from the way his body was pressed against hers. He wanted her to feel it. Get used to it.

He really did need to slow down, he thought, as he continued to kiss her. He would take things slow. This is what he wanted. What she wanted. And he was struck by the enormity of just how much passion was in one single kiss. Of how much tongue action was required. He was enjoying sharing both with her. There was nothing gentle about the kiss. Far from it.

There was hunger, gluttony, and a desperation he hadn't been used to before, but was getting familiar with now. For some reason she felt right in his arms. Right against his mouth. Right with her body pressed intimately against his.

It wasn't easy, but he finally gained control and pulled back. She gasped for breath the moment their mouths separated. After pulling air into his own lungs he leaned back close to her, lowered his head close to her ear and whispered in a deep, husky tone, "I like you. I like you a lot, but I can't force you to like me. All I can ask is that you give me a chance. Get to know me. The real me not the person that you think you know."

She rested her forehead on his chest. At first he wondered if she heard him, then he felt her sigh.

"What do you have to offer me?"

He sighed. "Take a chance and find out. I promise you. I will make it worth every moment of your time. I promise we will go slow, very slow. Now let's clean up, and you tell me what else you have planned for this evening."

She gave him a real smile, something that didn't happen often, and he felt like he had been kicked in the gut. Her smile was radiant and lit up her entire face.

"To be honest I don't have anything else planned. The original plan had been to feed you and put you out."

He chuckled when he realized she was serious. "I like your honesty," he replied brushing the back of his hand over her cheek.

"Are you ready for me to leave?"

She shook her head. "Not yet. How about we watch a movie?"

He wasn't ready to leave either. They hadn't reached an actual agreement yet, but she hadn't said no, and it was start.

"I like your idea."

After they cleaned up the kitchen she led the way into the living room and turned on the television. The first movie that she came across was *Pirates of the Caribbean*. She looked over at Eric.

"Is this okay?"

He nodded, and she put the remote down and settled in to watch the movie. They had only missed a few minutes of the movie. After the kiss they just shared he had to focus his mind to concentrate on the movie. Midway through the movie somehow they managed to become considerably close to each other. He smiled when she bravely removed the rest of the space separating them, and he automatically brought his arm up and placed it around her shoulder. She relaxed in his embrace, and it felt more natural than he thought it would, and they remained in that position until the movie ended.

Eric stretched as he looked at her. "I like that movie."

She smiled. "So do I, but then again, there aren't too many movies that I don't like."

He looked down at his watch. "Well hopefully we will have the opportunity to watch several more movies together."

She studied him for a moment and looked away but not before he saw the indecisiveness in her eyes. Her next words didn't do anything to assure him that tonight had made much of a difference. "We shall see."

Overall it had been a good night, and he wasn't going to push. After the kiss they just shared he knew he had proved there was chemistry between them. He would give her a little time and space to figure out her thoughts, her feelings. Standing up her held out his hand to her and pulled her to her feet.

"It is getting late, and I have errands that I need to run in the morning. However, the ball is in your court now. Call me when you are ready."

She nodded. "I will."

Her tone wasn't convincing, but he smiled. "Thank you for inviting me over. I'm not sure what made you do it, but I am glad."

"So am I," she replied softly.

He walked her to the front door before turning to face her. He leaned forward and gave her a brief kiss on the lips. "Good night and sweet dreams."

"You too," she whispered.

Eric opened the door and walked toward his SUV. When he reached it, he got in, and he saw that Keirra was still in the doorway watching him. He started the engine, and then Keirra closed the door. After backing out of the driveway, he made the short drive home.

It seemed strange to call it home, but it was. The time that he lived in Atlanta he had rented an apartment, but the move to Baxley made him want something more permanent. There had only been four houses available in Baxley that he'd been interested in, and the one that he bought was nice and had a homey feel to it. The house was also in a good position to be added onto or remodeled if needed. Right now, he liked it as it was. It was a one-story, four-bedroom, three-and-a-half bathroom house. Large enough for the family size that he wanted.

He walked into his house and went to his bedroom. He tossed his keys on the dresser and undressed. Once he was down to his boxers, he walked back into the living room. Stretching out on the couch he flipped on the television. He settled in to watch a little until he became sleepy.

He hadn't wanted to leave Keirra, but he hadn't wanted to wear out his welcome on the first visit. Also having her in his arms was almost more than he could handle, and the last thing he wanted was to make her anymore wary than she already was.

She was a character. Tonight had started out rocky but had quickly smoothed over. If he hadn't known better, he would have insisted that she had switched places with one of her sisters during the meal. The good thing was that she would fit right in with the family. His sisters could be neurotic as well. Gaia was the oldest of the four of them. Irene was the second oldest. Marianne was the third in birth order.

Growing up the only boy had been a lot of fun in a lot of ways, and traumatic in others. Either way he had learned valuable lessons from his sisters. He missed them, but he was happy in Baxley, and he knew that his family knew that now. It had almost started a riot when he had informed everyone that he was moving to Baxley. Since then, he had only been home once, but he was getting ready to go home twice and almost back-to-back. Next weekend was his mother's birthday, and Thanksgiving came around two weeks after that. Not to mention Christmas that would follow a month later.

Tomorrow was Halloween, so he had to get up and get some candy for the kids who would be on the hunt. Why he had waited until the last minute made no sense to him because he was normally more organized, but he was going to make the best of the situation. He would do a little last-minute decorating as well. By the time nightfall rolled around, he would be ready.

He turned onto the sports channel to catch the previews for upcoming games. Once the NFL previews were over, he turned off the television and headed for his bedroom.

Pulling back the covers, he crawled into bed and closed his eyes. The image of Keirra appeared before him so clearly that he had to open his eyes to make sure that she wasn't really there. He closed his eyes again. This time her image didn't appear, but his thoughts of her flowed freely. There was so much that he wanted to know about her.

Walking through the Smiths' house tonight, he had seen several pictures of the three sisters growing up. He had seen pictures of what he was certain were her parents and their grandparents as well, but he didn't know a lot about either of them because there was hardly any mention of them, at least to strangers.

One thing that he did know was that they were all deceased. When the time was right, he would ask. Keirra was a woman that he had to feel his way with. One wrong move, and he would be back to square one. He had made it this far, and he didn't feel like starting back over. A yawn escaped him, and he realized that sleepiness had sneaked up on him. He exhaled deeply before relaxing. Tomorrow was going to be a long day, and he needed his rest.

* * * *

"Okay, so what's up with you and Eric? I heard the two of you had dinner last night."

Keirra bit back a groan when Kristen asked the question as soon as they were seated at a booth in Sam's Café. The way she and her sisters ate at the restaurant they ought to have part ownership. Even so she had never eaten at Sam's so many times in one week. The food was excellent and reasonably priced for those who wanted a cheap meal, yet there were enough pricey items on the menu for those who wanted it.

Tonight she and Kristen were splurging. Instead of going for their normal food, they had both ordered thick juicy double cheeseburgers with bacon, and crisp waffle fries. When their burgers arrived they were on nice oversized plates, but the amount of food heaped on them took away from the size. They looked at each other and laughed. Keirra reached for the ketchup. "I think we should have just gotten one and split it."

Kristen shook her head. "Well, it is too late now. Besides I have a boyfriend at home who will finish what I can't eat. You would too if you gave Eric a chance."

Keirra took a bite of her burger and closed her eyes at the wonderful taste, and she took her time chewing giving herself time to collect her thoughts before she spoke.

"The man is sexy as hell, and it is irritating. I would love to go out with him, but I can't lower my guard. Every time I look at him I see dad, and it eats me up inside."

She wasn't even going to tell her sister about how he had rocked her world with his kiss. When he first lowered his head to kiss her, she had been set to resist, then his lips came down on hers, and she forgot what she was going to do. The man was a good kisser. No he was an excellent kisser. He made her forget where she was. She had no choice but to close her eyes, and her arms came up around his neck. The kiss seemed to go on forever. He wasn't aggressive, and he let her take the lead, but she realized that in several ways he still controlled the kiss.

When she pulled back and ended the kiss, she had felt different, different in a way that she couldn't explain at all. The storm of emotions that had rushed through her had frightened her. When Eric stepped away from her, she had shivered from his lack of warmth. She missed it even as she sat across from her sister pretending as though she didn't. She was way in over her head. This was starting to become more than a fear of Eric being an officer of the law. It was about what he could do to her if she let him.

Kristen stared at Keirra a long time before speaking. "You have to get over this unnatural fear at some point. I'm not going to lie. I do think about Randy getting hurt on the job, and when he is serving a warrant, I'm almost beside myself. I also think about what happened to dad a lot, but my love for Randy won't let me turn away from him. I can't."

Keirra smiled. "Does Randy know you love him?"

Kristen grinned, and Keirra was a little jealous at her sister's obvious joy. "I tell him everyday."

Keirra frowned. "So you think I should give Eric a chance?"

Kristen nodded. "From what I know about Eric he's a great guy. He has come over to the house and hung out a few times with us. I like him."

Keirra was still skeptical, and her next statement proved it. "You know my history with men."

Kristen laughed. "Yes, I do, but everyone has had a bad relationship or two. The point is to invent a new mistake not repeat the old ones. You know what you have done wrong in the past, so learn from it."

Keirra rolled her eyes. "All of my relationships have been disasters, Kristen. I have chosen men like Eric in the past, and it hasn't worked out."

Kristen shook her head. "I disagree. Eric is nothing like any of the men you have dated in the past. If you let down your guard and get to know him, you will see that. Try to be a little nicer, a little more approachable. Don't assume he is like the men you have encountered in the past."

Keirra laughed when she thought of a few of her past boyfriends. "Do you remember Daniel?"

Kristen choked on her waffle fry before looking up at Keirra with a horrified expression. Daniel had been a guy who had been interested in Keirra, or at least they thought so. The creep had taken a pass at all three of them under the false pretense he couldn't tell the three of them apart. Turned out Daniel had been a man whose sole purpose in life was to get laid by as many women possible.

"He is a perfect example of what Daniel isn't. Heck, Eric can already tell us apart."

Keirra smiled. "So you noticed that, too?"

Kristen took another bite of her burger before speaking. "You would have to be insane not to. There are people here who have known us for a long time and still can't tell us apart."

"True."

"So what do you have against getting involved with Eric?"

Keirra smiled. "It isn't the date I would mind. It's Eric. He is too intense. Too overbearing, irritating, confident and—"

"Sexy as sin," Kristen supplied with a smile.

Keirra rolled her eyes. Another prospective date with Eric bothered her. She didn't know if she could hold on to her self-control around him. What troubled her even more was Eric wasn't going to give up on her. Her sister was right. She did deserve happiness and a good man. She just wasn't sure the man was Eric. She focused on her burger and tried to formulate a plan to deal with Eric. She hadn't so far, and it was frustrating.

Kristen dredged her French fry through the ketchup with an innocent look on her face, Keirra didn't buy for one instant. "So you do realize you still haven't given me one good reason why you shouldn't go out with Eric?"

Keirra shook her head at her sister before looking away. "And I don't know why you won't leave this alone."

"Because I think you are walking away from the man who is perfect for you, and you don't realize it."

Keirra looked at her sister with wide eyes. Was she supposed to believe Eric was the man for her? If he was it would serve her right, but for as much of her life as she had spent trying to avoid men in uniforms, for her to end up with one would be too much. Could fate be so cruel? She refused to fall for Eric if she could help it. It would be an absolute dating disaster, and at this point in her life, she had already had enough to last her a lifetime.

"You know you can't avoid the inevitable forever, don't you?"

Keirra scowled at her sister's dramatics. "I'm not avoiding anything."

How could she avoid something that didn't exist?

Kristen shook her head, picking up another waffle fry. "The sad thing is you believe that for some strange and demented reason."

Keirra nodded and smiled knowing she would soon be getting to the end of her sister's high level of patience, which meant she could go home and lock herself in her room. Unless she could get out here at a reasonable time she would have to go home and deal with Kayla. Her oldest sister was out with Lucas, but she was hoping to beat her back to the house.

She sighed. Both of her sisters were driving her nuts about Eric. She was almost to the point that if she heard the man's name again she was going to scream.

Kristen took a bite of her burger and chewed slowly. When she finished she tilted her head to the side with an inquisitive expression. "Why don't you just admit you want Eric and you would love to go out with him?"

Keirra rolled her eyes again, but when they fell on the man who had just walked through the door she averted her gaze and began to contemplate ways to get out of Sam's without being seen. Somehow, she knew it was going to be difficult.

She wasn't ready to see him yet. Yes, she had thought about him ever since he left her home last night, but seeing him here, so soon, so unexpectedly, was too much.

"Are you going to answer me?"

Keirra jumped before looking at her sister and shaking her head. "No, but I am going to try to get our bill so we can leave."

Kristen gave her a puzzled look. "What's wrong with you?"

Before Keirra could answer, she laid eyes on Eric, and the corners of her mouth curved upward. "Ah, there is the man of the hour."

Before she could stop her, Kristen called out to Eric. When he turned in their direction, Keirra wanted to crawl under the table.

"I hate you," she whispered before Eric was in hearing distance. Kristen just laughed and asked Eric to join them. He chose to slide in the booth beside her, and she closed her eyes in displeasure. Kristen and Eric seemed to be intent on ignoring her.

"What brings you here tonight?"

Eric gave Kristen his heart-stopping grin. "I just got off work and decided to run here to grab a bite to eat before heading home."

She smiled in relief. "Well don't let us keep you. You look like you're in a rush."

Lord, she hoped he was, because if he sat there much longer she might not be responsible for her actions.

Kristen looked over at Eric and chuckled. "You have to excuse my sister. She is a little upset at being attracted to you."

"I'm not attracted to him," Keirra growled angrily, trying not to think about the bone-melting kiss, or the embarrassing statement her sister just made.

Kristen continued on as if Keirra hadn't spoken. "I told her I think dating you would be a good thing, but for some reason she doesn't believe me. I know you don't know a lot of people in town. Maybe you can talk Keirra into being a good neighbor and giving you a tour around town."

Kristen began to search through her purse until she found her wallet. She put enough money on the table to cover her meal and a nice tip before giving her sister an innocent smile. "It is getting late, and I just remembered I have an errand I need to run before I head home."

Keirra's mouth dropped open. "In case you forgot I rode with you."

Kristen grinned. "I am sure Eric won't mind being a nice neighbor and giving you a ride home."

Kristen turned and almost sprinted toward the door. It took Keirra a minute to respond to her sister's irrational behavior. She couldn't wait to get home if she made it home anytime soon. The look in Eric's gaze told her he might not let her out of his sight for a while.

If Kristen thought she was off the hook, she had another thing coming. She was going to get an earful. Closing her eyes she sighed and turned her attention to the man who had been nothing but a pain in her side.

"What the hell has gotten into her?"

His eyebrows rose at her question. "I have been wondering the same thing about you."

She looked at Eric in surprise. "Don't start with me. It is obvious that I have enough mentally deranged people in my life. I don't need to add you to the group."

Eric chuckled as he slid out of the booth and moved around to sit across from her. Her eyes widened, and she wondered if he heard anything she just said, or what she had been saying since she met him. "I guess not, but I would like to know why you are so against us going out?"

She crossed her arms over her chest. "I say we just forget the whole thing."

His smile widened. "I can't say I have ever been one to give up without a fight."

She frowned and watched him snag a fry off of her plate. "I think this is one fight you should give up."

He finished chewing and laughed. "You might be right. You make dating you sound like torture."

She would have told him it was torture but the waitress walked up and took his order. When he requested for it to be made to go, she looked at him with surprise. She had heard him say he was stopping by to pick up some food, but she hadn't believed him. She was certain he had made up the excuse just to find a reason to join her. But he hadn't. He wouldn't have even known she was in here anyway. She wasn't in her car.

She felt insulted, and she didn't know why. Maybe she was starting to suffer from the same delusion running in her family because she did want him to stay and join her. She didn't know how much until she found out he wasn't. Eating dinner with him last night had been more fun than she thought it would be. She wanted that again and soon. But she was afraid to ask for it in a way. Afraid of what it would represent if she did.

"You aren't going to stay and eat?"

He shook his head. "I told you I was just stopping by to grab something to eat. I need to get home because there are a few things I need to do before I go to bed. I had a taste for enchiladas, and though my mom would kill me for saying it, Sam's makes very good enchiladas."

Keirra stared at him. Why had she thought he had come here for her? More importantly, why did it bother her that he hadn't? As soon as she asked herself the question she knew the answer. Yet, she couldn't bring herself to admit it, and she hoped she would never have to.

She paused a moment trying to contemplate all of the possible outcomes. When she could think of more outcomes that were positive than negative she knew that she would be a fool not to give him a chance. She wanted to get to know him better. Spend time with him. She looked across the table at Eric, but he was staring out the window. Reaching across the table she touched his hand.

He didn't bother to hide his surprise when he looked over at her.

"Is something wrong?"

She shook her head. "No. If you don't have any pressing plans, I would really like it if you would stay and have dinner with me."

He stared at her for what seemed like forever. When he raised his hands to capture the attention of the waitress she pulled her hand back unsure of what to expect. When the waitress came up to the table, Eric spoke to her without breaking eye contact with Keirra.

"Could you change my order from take-out to dine-in? It looks like I will be staying after all."

Chapter Four

"Tell me about your family."

Eric swallowed the bite of food he had just eaten. He had been surprised by Keirra's impromptu invite to stay and join her for dinner. In all truthfulness, he was surprised that she wanted to spend time with him again so quickly. But he wasn't complaining.

"Well, my mom and dad have been happily married for forty years. They met in my mother's homeland of Puerto Rico while Dad was in the military." Eric's lips curved upward. "Two years later, they married, and my dad brought her here to the States."

Eric took another bite of food, chewed, and swallowed it before he told her about his sisters, their husbands, and their children. Kristen laughed at a few of his stories. After that, they ate in silence until he noticed Keirra was staring at him intently. She was obviously thinking, and he wanted to know what about.

"What is it?"

She smiled. "Do you think that we are drawn to each other because we have so much in common?"

He leaned back in the booth. "Like what?"

"Mainly, we are stubborn and used to getting our way because we are both spoiled."

Eric grinned, flashing her with his perfectly straight teeth. He was willing to admit his faults if she was willing to admit hers.

"I think that it helps, but don't discount your intelligence and beauty."

Keirra rolled her eyes before smiling. "You have a tongue like butter."

The look in Eric's eyes darkened. "Trust me it isn't made of butter, and I will be more than willing to show you later."

He saw her shiver in reaction to his words, but she wouldn't let her gaze waver, and the corner's of his mouth tilted upward. He liked that she didn't shy away from his attraction to her, the intensity of it. He had a lot of energy, and he needed a woman that could keep up with him. In his opinion, Keirra was that woman.

She shifted in her seat before replying. "Have you been to Puerto Rico?"

He nodded. "Yes I have, several times as matter of fact. My mother still has a lot of family there."

"What is it like there?"

Eric's mouth curled upward at Keirra's question. "It is too beautiful for me to describe with words. Maybe we will get the chance to get there one of these days."

He read the surprise in her eyes. "My statement shouldn't surprise you, Keirra, because understand something, when I am with a woman who I am serious about, she knows it. I am serious about you."

Keirra's eyes widened. "Have you cared about a lot of women?"

Eric nodded. "I have cared about all of them."

Uncertainty flickered in her eyes, and he hid his amusement. Eric took another bite of his food before chewing. He wanted to let her think about her statement. Somehow he hadn't managed to convince her that he was a one-woman man, but he would.

After he swallowed, he spoke again. He wanted to put her fears at ease. "I have cared about every woman I have dated, enough to be selective about who I actually choose as well as to treat each and every one of them with the respect every woman deserves, but that is where the comparison between you and them ends." Eric smiled. "You make me wait to give you things that I would give no other woman."

She remained silent, but her eyes, her expression, told him she was thinking. He wanted to know what was on her mind. "What are you thinking about?"

Keirra looked up from her plate. "I am thinking about all of the reasons why I shouldn't date you," she replied honestly.

Eric laughed. "I like that about you. Your honesty is a turn on to me."

Keirra rolled her eyes at the comment, and he chuckled. "I am serious."

"I know," she replied dryly.

He chuckled. "Tell me about your family."

Keirra shrugged. "You know most of them. The only people you haven't met are my paternal grandparents."

Keirra told him about them. The smile on his face had widened by the time she was finished. "What about your parents?"

As soon as the words were out of his mouth, he knew that he had made a mistake. Keirra's body language changed completely. "Maybe some other time."

Her tone spoke of finality, and he didn't press the subject. Yet, there was something about the Smith sisters' past that had caused them a lot of pain. He knew that was a part of the reason as to why Keirra had avoided him up until this point. Until he discovered what the devastating secret was, he knew he wouldn't get to know the real Keirra. That bothered him because he really did care a lot about Keirra. Most of their relationship had consisted of him chasing her and her avoiding him at all costs.

He laughed at the thought of some of the interactions that occurred between the two of them and frowned at others. One of the things that he liked about her was she had a mouth on her, and she wasn't afraid to use it. Keirra had either cursed at him or cursed because of him so many times it was downright humorous. He liked a woman who could stand her ground and demand what she wanted. Keirra was the woman he wanted in his life. Now he had to convince her that was what he wanted.

* * * *

Eric dialed his parents' phone number and smiled. He loved them for everything that they had done for him. Everything that they had given him, and everything that they had made him work hard for. His mother answered the phone on the second ring.

"Hello Mom—"

He was interrupted by his mother's rapid secession of Spanish. She scolded him for going so long without calling.

Eric laughed. "Well, Mom, I have been a little busy."

"When have you ever been too busy to call your parents?" his mother questioned him with puzzlement.

Eric chuckled. "Since I have been busy pursuing a woman who I am really interested in."

His mother was silent for a moment before speaking. "Well don't keep me waiting. Tell me about her."

He launched into the story of his first meeting with Keirra and of everything that had happened since. By the time he finished, his mother was laughing.

"Well, son, it seems as if you have met your match."

He had to smile himself as he thought about Keirra. "I know. That is a part of the reason that I am attracted to her. She isn't a doormat. She wouldn't be a woman who does something just because I say do it or to keep me. And she isn't worried about impressing me. She is comfortable in her skin. Secure in who she is as a person."

"Well from what you have told me, she sounds like a nice woman."

Eric's smile grew. "She is, and that is why I want you guys to meet her."

Eric sat back and listened to his mother as she shot off another round of rapid Spanish. When his mother finished, he shook his head.

"Well, don't get too excited. I still have to ask her if she would like to come."

His mother sighed with impatience. "Make sure you use every ounce of persuasion you have in your body."

Eric laughed. "Okay, Mom. I will."

"Make sure that you do, and give me a call back to let me know what her answer is as soon as you have it."

"How late are you going to be up?"

"At least another hour."

He grinned. "That should be enough time to convince her."

"Well, hurry up and call her."

Eric said bye to his mother with the promise to call her back in an hour either way it turned out. He took a deep breath before dialing Keirra's number.

In the short time he had the number he had memorized it. Keirra answered the phone on the third ring. She sounded a bit winded.

He smiled. "Did I catch you at a bad time?"

He heard her take a deep breath before continuing. "No I just couldn't find the phone. I think Kayla hid it again."

Eric laughed as Keirra grumbled about Kayla having a bad habit of doing that. He would bet everything he had that growing up with the Smith sisters had been a blast. They were so full of life. He knew many people thought highly of them around Baxley.

"Well, I called you for good reason."

Keirra laughed. "I would hope so. I have never been a fan of bad news."

"Well, the reason that I called you is that this weekend is my mother's birthday, and I would really like it if you could join me in Atlanta for her party."

Her silence told him he shocked her, and when her voice came out in a croak, it was confirmed. She cleared her throat. "Are you sure that you want me to go? I mean we hardly know each other."

He chuckled. "We know each other well enough. I am very sure I want you to come to Atlanta with me."

Keirra paused. "Who else is going to be there?"

He smiled before reclining back on the couch. "My parents as well as my sisters and their families."

"So in other words, your *entire* family," she said on a groan.

Eric laughed. "Oh no. Not my entire family by any means. Just in case I didn't tell you. My mother is one of twelve, and my father is one of six."

Her gasp of surprise traveled across the phone line, and he could tell he shocked her with the information. From his conversations with Randy, he knew Keirra and her sisters craved the closeness of a family. He hoped she would say yes to meeting his family. She would fit in well, and his mother would love her. He waited anxiously for her to give him an answer. She was taking longer than he would like to say yes and he wasn't certain she would. He had to figure out something he could say or do to convince her.

Just as he went to speak, she took a deep breath, and his heart rate slowed in disappointment as he realized she was going to turn him down.

"As crazy as I think this idea is, and as nervous as I am about meeting your family, I would love to go with you to Atlanta."

He couldn't express the happiness he felt at her words, but he should have known she would accept. He'd issued a challenge. He wasn't surprised that she was willing to face the challenge head on. He was willing to admit that he didn't think it would be this easy. Nothing with her ever was. It was one of the things that attracted him to her. Maybe Kristen had been right in stating that all he had to do was challenge Keirra to capture her interest. Now he had to figure out what to do to keep it.

Chapter Five

Keirra took another sip of her coffee as she turned off the engine and grabbed her bag before climbing out. Unfortunately, the weekend had flown by, entirely too quickly. It was another Monday, and that meant it was the beginning of another workweek. She walked into the building with her best smile in place. She signed in then went to her classroom. The first bell of the day rang, and the rest of the day flew by. Before she knew it the day was over. She straightened up her classroom before heading to the front office to sign out.

Thankfully, the drive home was a short one. She pulled into the driveway before heading into the house. Kayla hadn't made it home yet, so she would have the house to herself for a few minutes. That gave her time to go upstairs and relax for a little while. She and her sisters would all be meeting at Sam's Café in an hour or two. Their routine was to meet at Sam's Café every Monday for dinner. So far, that routine hadn't been broken. There had been a time when they vowed not to eat at the restaurant, but that vow had gone out the window the next week. They were addicted to Sam's Café, and there wasn't anything that would keep them away from weekly Monday dinner. Sure they could meet at the house and have dinner there, but it wasn't Sam's Café. Sam's Café held memories for them that could never be replaced.

She walked into her room and sat her bag down by the dresser. Right now, she had no idea of what she was going to wear, but she would figure it out before it was time to leave. She slipped out of her shoes before walking over to her closet. Her style was definitely one of comfort and casual. She wasn't one who wanted to walk around uncomfortable all day long just to keep up with modern fashion. Fashion was something that she could create on her own. After opening the door to her closet, she began to flip through her clothes. She chose her favorite relaxed fit denim jeans and paired it up with a blue print pointelle V-neck shirt. Satisfied with the outfit she laid it aside before sitting on the edge of her bed. A quick glance at the clock told her that she had made good time in picking out her outfit.

A yawn escaped her, and she made the decision to take a power nap. She set the alarm for thirty minutes before lying down. When it went off, she wished she had set it for longer. She turned it off before getting out of bed. Thankfully it didn't take her long to get ready because she was starving. By the time she made it downstairs, Kayla was already in the living room waiting for her.

"Did you have a good nap?"

Kayla nodded. "Yes I did, only it wasn't long enough."

She was tired from getting up so early this morning. It had been her workout morning, so she had to get up in time enough to work out, take a shower, and eat breakfast. It was a routine that she followed at least three days a week as well as four before and after the holidays. She and her sisters took pleasure in their food. Even though that was the case, they tried to eat as healthy as possible as well as work out. Since she had been back in Baxley she had done very well.

"Hopefully, I won't be this tired tomorrow," she murmured as she followed Kayla to the front door.

Kayla groaned. "Well I am sure I will be since tomorrow is my day to work out."

Keirra smiled as they walked to Kayla's car. If she had to run two miles, there was no question she would be tired.

As athletic as she was, she despised running. She would do it if she had to, but only if her life was in danger. If she had a choice, she wasn't running anywhere. She got into the car, and Kayla drove them to Sam's Café. Kristen pulled up at the same time that they did. Keirra couldn't stop the grin that appeared on her face. She embraced her younger sister before locking arms with her. They headed into the restaurant together. Once they were seated and their drink orders were taken, their normal conversation resumed.

"So how was everyone's Monday?"

Keirra laughed at her younger sister's question. "You know we always ask each other that question every Monday, and so far I don't think that the answer has ever changed."

Kristen shrugged. "It is habit, but I also ask because you never know when the answer might change."

Nadia came up to their table and sat their drinks down. They all gave their orders after a quick glance at the menu. When Nadia left, Kristen turned her attention back to Keirra.

"Besides I wanted to talk to you about your dinner date with Eric."

Keirra found herself rolling her eyes. "I just bet you do, but you don't get an explanation since you abandoned me here with him."

Kayla looked back and forth between both of her sisters. "Where was I?"

Keirra arched a dark brow in Kayla's direction. "Out with your boyfriend Lucas."

Kayla frowned. "It's not like that. Lucas and I have only been out a few times, and it doesn't seem to be going anywhere, so it was probably the last time."

Kristen reached for her drink. "Well just look at it this way. I owed you one since you were bold enough to hang up on me."

Keirra had known that was coming. She was surprised that Kristen hadn't mentioned it before. "Well maybe if the two of you weren't so insensitive about the situation. At the time I—"

Keirra paused as Kayla choked on her soda. Kristen patted her on the back, and Kayla recovered slowly.

"You have to excuse me. I didn't know that you knew the meaning of the word."

Keirra felt irritation surge through her. "Don't forget that you haven't had your turn yet."

Kayla shrugged. "I welcome your meddling when it is my turn."

Keirra rolled her eyes. "You say that now, but we will see."

Kayla sighed heavily. "Yes. Hopefully we will."

Keirra heard the longing in her sister's voice. She gave Kayla's hand a reassuring pat. "If there is someone out there for me, there has to be someone out therefore you."

"You have got that right," Kristen added.

That earned her a nasty look from Keirra, and Kristen held her hands up. "I was just agreeing with you."

"With a little too much enthusiasm if you ask me."

They were interrupted as Nadia brought their food to the table. As soon as they were alone again, Kayla began to laugh. Keirra looked at oldest sister certain she had lost her mind.

"What is so funny?"

Kayla shook her head. "I miss this. It is so fun to have us together again and arguing like we used to do."

Keirra smiled. "You have no idea how strange that sounded, but I know exactly what you mean."

When they were able to stop laughing, they began eating. They were halfway through with their meal before anyone spoke again.

Keirra took a drink of her soda before speaking. She might as well bring up what she had agreed to with Eric. Her sisters were going to get her for not mentioning it right away as it was.

"I thought you guys might be interested in knowing that Eric invited me to Atlanta for his mother's birthday party."

This time, it was Kristen's turn to choke. Kayla patted Kristen on the back while giving Keirra a flabbergasted look.

"I knew there was something you were keeping from me."

Keirra shrugged and resumed eating. Kristen was finally able to stop choking.

"Oh no, ma'am. You don't say something like that then pretend like it isn't anything."

Keirra smiled. She had held off on telling them because she was still torn about the trip. Going back to Atlanta would bring up a lot of feelings for her. Neither she nor her sisters had ever been back. As sad as it was to say, they were afraid to go back. She still was. There was no telling what kind of feelings she would have of being in Atlanta would bring up. Yet she was dying to meet Eric's family, and she had no idea why. She looked up at her sisters.

"You should also keep in mind that I didn't have to tell you."

Kristen laughed. "You wouldn't have been able to keep it secret for long."

Keirra grinned. She never realized how much fun it could be to torture her sisters. Normally she did it for their own good, but tonight it was for fun.

"Maybe. Maybe not."

Kayla folded her arms. "What I want to know is what your reply was."

Keirra paused for dramatic flair. "I told him yes."

The silence that followed was entertaining to Keirra, but no more than her sisters' expressions. Her sisters knew the significance of her returning to Atlanta after all of these years.

Finally Kristen shook her head. "I'm sorry, but I don't believe I heard you correctly."

Keirra took another bite of her food before pushing her plate away. "No, you heard me correctly. Eric invited me to Atlanta, and I accepted."

Kristen turned to look at Kayla. "Have you been poisoning her?"

Keirra laughed. She didn't know what she would do without her sisters' sense of humor. She didn't know what she would do without them, period. There were times when she was certain that people thought they had truly lost their minds. The sad thing was that they hadn't. This came natural for them. Smiling at her sisters, she decided to put them out of their misery. She launched into the events that had occurred between Eric and her that led up to him inviting her to his mother's birthday party. Her sisters' mouths were hanging open in disbelief by the time she finished.

Kayla recovered first. She cleared her throat, picking up her fork. "So when are you guys leaving?"

Keirra groaned at the reminder. "Early Saturday morning. Extremely early."

Kristen shrugged. "Well at least you will be having fun."

Keirra gave her sister a puzzled look. "How do you figure that?"

Kristen grinned. "Well you have to look at the man that Eric is."

Kayla nodded. "Besides, most people who don't think highly of their family tend to hide them."

Keirra was compelled to agree. Both of her sisters had very good points. Her sisters had also given her the last reassurance that she needed to be completely okay with this trip to Atlanta. She looked over at her sisters with a genuine smile on her face.

"Thank you."

Neither one of them had to ask why she was thanking them. Because of the bond that they shared, the look in her eyes told them everything that they needed to know.

Chapter Six

"Wait . . . I have changed my mind."

She watched with irritation as Eric smiled as he placed Keirra's bag in the backseat and closed the door. She was still nervous about the drive to Atlanta to meet his family. The idea of the trip brought up so many memories for her. Ones she wasn't quite ready to face. Now that they were getting ready to pull off, she was having second thoughts. It was something he must have expected because he put the last bag in the car before looking at her patiently.

"You said you want to get to know me better. What better way than through my family?"

Keirra groaned in agony. "Why does everything I say come back to hunt me?"

He laughed. "Are you afraid my family will attack at the first sight of blood? If so, I could invite Kayla along as well. She could be the distraction you need."

She growled at him for saying something so ridiculous, and he smiled. "You know I like it when you make that sound."

She rolled her eyes. "I'm going to ignore that statement, and inviting Kayla along won't help. If anything it would make things worse."

Even as she said it, she was sure that Eric was aware of that, which was probably why he suggested it. Sighing in defeat, she dropped her shoulders, and his smile widened.

"Well, then I say we should go now."

He walked around to the passenger side of his car and opened the door. She looked back at the house longingly but knew that there was no reason for her not to go. She slid into the car. Eric closed the door, went around to the driver's side, and got in.

"This is going to be a lot of fun."

Keirra wasn't so sure. Meeting a man's family wasn't something that was normally done after the first date. Which in all reality might not have qualified as a date according to her sisters. Either way it seemed that she was getting herself talked into a lot of things that she should think about more carefully before agreeing to them, this trip to Atlanta being one of the prime examples as to why she should.

Sighing she closed her eyes and laid her head back against the headrest. The lack of sleep that she had due to her tossing and turning plus it was four in the morning. She didn't even wake up this early to go to work. The earliest that she had ever gotten up was six. She taught seventh-and eighth-grade math in middle school. It was interesting on a day-to-day basis. There was never a dull day with her students. She didn't remember middle school being that interesting or traumatic.

She loved what she did, and she wouldn't change that for the world. Bringing her hand up to her mouth she hid a yawn but the lull of the car's motion and her tiredness won, and within minutes she was asleep. What seemed like minutes later Eric was waking her gently.

She raised the chair to its original position and gasped. The house she stared at was massive and in the nice part of Atlanta.

She looked over at him. "You didn't tell me you were rich. No wonder you gave me that look when I accused you of being spoiled."

He chuckled. "I figured you didn't need another reason to tell me no. You already accused me of being spoiled, and besides I'm not rich. My parents are."

She hit him in the arm playfully. "Well you are very used to getting your way."

Her gaze went back to the house that could only be described as a mansion. He got out of the car and came around to her side. She stepped out when he opened the door.

He chuckled. "Which has more to do with me being the youngest of four and the only boy versus being rich. Now, let's get inside. My parents are probably still asleep, and everyone else won't be here until a few hours from now."

"What time is it?"

"A little after nine."

He grabbed their bags, and she followed him to the house. She watched as he shifted the bags to use his key. They stepped inside, and she gasped.

He smiled. "I will give you a tour of the house later. I promise."

She nodded, and he led the way to one of the guest rooms. "This is where you will sleep tonight."

He walked into the spacious room and sat her bag on the chair. "If you need me I'll be two doors down the hall on the right."

She hardly heard him because she was still amazed by the room and the house. "Get some more rest," she murmured.

He closed the door, and she went to her bag. She was still sleepy, but she was too wired to sleep. After opening her bag, she began to pull out her clothes. She found the space to put them up. The second thing that she had to decide was if she was going to change or not. It seemed like it was going to be a warm day. She decided to keep her blue jeans on, but she was going to change shirts. Once she figured which shirt she was going to change into, she pulled out her pajama pants and a matching camisole to sleep in. When she finally climbed into the bed, she moaned. The mattress was firm just like she liked it. Maybe she could go back to sleep after all.

* * * *

Keirra pulled her hair up into a ponytail. She arranged the ponytail into one thick braid and put a ponytail holder around the end of it.

"Are you sure I look okay?"

The corners of his mouth curled upward. "Yes, I am."

She took a deep breath to relax. It seemed everyone had arrived, and now it was her time to meet and greet. He took her hands in his.

"My family is going to love you, and you are going to love them."

She exhaled a nervous breath. "Okay."

He led the way out of the guest room and down the hallway. "Let me know when you are ready for your tour."

She nodded, and he led her through the foyer and finally to the kitchen. "Where are we going?"

"Everyone is outside in the backyard."

He continued to a glass door that led out to the backyard. She gasped in amazement again. The backyard was massive. There was a pool and a large covered seating area with several people already under it. She had to turn in a complete circle to take everything in. Suddenly it seemed everyone knew she appeared. All of their gazes fell on her, and she unconsciously took a step back. He held onto her.

"Don't worry. If they bite you, I will bite them back."

He tightened his grip on her as he led her toward the covered area. His firm grip was reassuring. So many things about him were. Someone called out to him.

"Hey, Eric, are you going to introduce us to your *girlfriend*, or are you going to keep her to yourself?"

She looked at Eric in surprise as he shot something back in Spanish before finishing in English.

"Wait your turn, Gaia."

Keirra felt her skin tingle, and her heart rate speed up a little. Eric had a way with words that did something to her. She didn't know if it was his voice or his accent when he switched over to Spanish, but he sounded so sexy when he spoke that it was sinful. Yet, since deciding to get to know him, she was starting find out there was a lot more to Eric than she would have ever guessed. In some ways it concerned her. She didn't want to let her guard down too quickly with Eric. He had been right with his assumption in that he had the potential to hurt her in a way no other man had. The thought was enough to send a sliver of panic through her. It was one of the main reasons why she had avoided him as long as she had. Eric made her nervous. He represented passion, passion that she had yet to experience. She was pulled from her internal rambling when he squeezed her hand again.

He led her in the direction of his parents. They were a lovely couple, and Keirra got a good idea of how Eric was going to look when he was older. His looks were only going to improve. Arthur was a very nice-looking man. Eric had gotten his dark hair and his height from his father. He had gotten his skin complexion and eyes from his mother.

"Mom, Dad, this is Keirra. Keirra, this is my mom and dad, Arthur and Charlotte."

Keirra shivered as she heard Eric's mother's name roll off of his tongue. His accent was coming out, and she decided she needed to warn him about his use of it in front of her. She knew his ego didn't need the boosting, but it was either she tell him or suffer in silence.

He tugged her forward when his patents stood. They each embraced her warmly. "It is a pleasure to meet you. Our son has told us a lot about you."

She gave Eric a pointed look. "Hopefully good things."

Charlotte laughed. "Of course, dear. I hope that my children and grandchildren are on their best behavior and you enjoy yourself."

She made the statement loud enough for everyone to hear. There were a few groans.

"Darn, there goes our plan," one of his sisters responded.

Charlotte patted her arm reassuringly. "Don't worry. They are just kidding."

Eric took her hand in his. "Come on. Let's meet the rest of these crazy people that I call family."

He led her closer to the tent and introduced her to the family. Gaia and her husband Owen were introduced to her first along with their children Yvonne, Bianca, and Daniel. They all greeted her with smiles. She was introduced to Marianne and Wyatt next. Their two daughters Fallyn and Nina were adorable. Irene and Scott and their three boys Howard, Joel, and Lance were the last part of the family she was introduced to. Irene was the one who made the statement earlier.

She thought that they were a beautiful family. With the introductions over Nina ran over to her uncle.

"Is it time for my piggyback ride," she asked as she bounced back and forth anxiously.

Eric looked over at Keirra. "Will you be okay?"

She nodded. With sisters like hers she should be able to survive his. "I will be fine."

He knelt down, and his youngest niece jumped onto his back. Eric shot off as soon as he was sure they both had a good grip on each other. Marianne shouted in rapid Spanish at the both of them, and she saw Eric slow down a little. She looked up at Keirra with a smile.

"Have a seat and join us."

Keirra found a vacant seat at the end of the table and sat down. A few minutes later, she found out that Eric was right. His family wasn't that bad. They didn't even interrogate, and she had been sure she was going to receive one. Eric was lucky to have the family that he had. They were funny, outgoing, and witty.

It was fun to sit back and watch them banter with each other. Eric appeared by her side holding his niece. Nina couldn't have been anymore than six years of age. Eric took a seat beside her with his niece in his lap. Keirra's heart leaped at the sight. It was the first time that she had ever thought about him with children. Now that she saw him in action, she could picture it clearly. He was very attentive, somehow managing to give his niece, her, and his sisters his attention. She watched Nina become bored and climb down out of her uncle's lap. The little girl ran off to play with her sister and cousins, and Keirra had to fight the urge to climb into Eric's lap herself.

"I say that we play a game of Bullshit."

Keirra looked up a surprise. A deck of cards appeared.

Eric leaned closer to her. "Do you know how to play?"

"I think that I had friends that played it in college."

He chuckled before explaining it to her. The game was very familiar to what she had seen in college. Although she couldn't recall who it was she had seen play it. The game went slow, and it was because no one was really concentrating on it. They were too busy telling jokes and making fun of each other, but it was fun, too much fun. By the time Irene won, Keirra was holding her sides because they hurt so badly from laughing. The Brooks gang was hilarious, and Eric was right. She did feel like she fitted right in with everyone. If there was anyone that had a personality similar to hers it was Irene. Irene exhibited the same dry wit that she did. They seemed to connect the most, and at one time had double-teamed on everyone.

"Anyone up for a swim," Marianne asked.

"Oh yeah," Wyatt replied as he stood up.

"I can never remember a time growing up when we would still be able to get in the pool at this time of year," Gaia murmured as she stood.

Everyone murmured their agreement as they stood up and headed for the house. Keirra was sort of surprised at how hot it was. It was a good day for a swim. She went into the guest room and pulled out the three swimsuits that she had chosen to bring upon Eric's instructions. She grinned when she looked at the raspberry colored bikini. It was her favorite. The bikini covered up the most yet it revealed what she needed it to. She began to strip and put on the swimsuit.

At the last minute she decided to put on a sarong. Parading through the Brooks house half naked was the last impression that she wanted to make. Walking over to the mirror, she wrapped her ponytail into a ball and pinned it. The chlorine wasn't good for her hair. With one last glimpse in the mirror, she exited the room and ran right into Marianne.

"Oops."

"Sorry."

Marianne locked arms with her. "No problem. Although I am sure Eric wouldn't mind having one less sister."

Keirra laughed. "Well believe it or not he loves you guys and wouldn't trade any of you for anything."

Marianne smiled in return. "Believe it or not we wouldn't trade him for anything either."

Marianne led her back through the house and outside. They were the last to arrive at the pool. There was a natural sparkle of friendliness in Marianne's eyes when she looked at Keirra.

"Well I hope that you are enjoying yourself."

Keirra found herself smiling. "I am, and thank you for making me feel at home."

Keirra looked around and hoped that she looked half as good as Gaia, Irene, and Marianne did after having kids. Her attention slowly went in Eric's direction. Keirra felt her mouth go dry. The man was good looking with clothes on. He was even sexier without them. Now she could see the muscles she had felt so often. She had to avert her gaze before she made a fool of herself.

Owen was the first to slide into the pool. Everyone began to follow him in. Keirra walked over to the edge of the pool and sat down. She slid her feet into the water. A laugh escaped her as she saw Gaia and Owen share a quick kiss before she dunked him. Marianne and Wyatt were floating together side by side, and Irene and Scott were swimming around the pool together. It made her wonder if she would share anything like that with Eric, but even if she didn't, whoever did would be lucky.

Chapter Seven

Keirra let out a shriek of terror as Eric appeared in front of her without warning. He chuckled as she placed a hand to her rapidly rising chest.

"Good Lord, Eric, you nearly scared me to death."

He swam closer to her. "Sorry. I didn't mean to."

Reaching for her legs, he tugged her closer to the edge of the pool. "Why aren't you in the swimming pool?"

She smiled. "I'm not good at swimming."

A look of surprise appeared on his face. "Yeah right. You not good at something?"

She stuck her tongue out at him. "Yes, I'm not perfect, you know. Trust me, dog paddling is the best that I can do."

He laughed in response. "Well, I want you to come into the water with me."

She shook head. Her last intention was to get into the water. She really was a bad swimmer even in the shallow end. As athletic as she was, water was her one weakness.

"I will hold on to you."

She laughed. If that was supposed to reassure her, he had another thing coming. He must have interpreted her thoughts.

"I won't drown you, nor will I let you drown yourself. I promise."

He held up his hand in what she guessed was supposed to be Scout's honor. It only took her a minute to decide that she really did want to get in the pool. She hadn't been in one in years.

"Okay, but I want to get in on the shallow end."

He nodded and swam in the other direction of the pool. Keirra allowed herself to enjoy the ripples of his back and arm muscles as he moved through the water. She stood up and walked down to the shallow end. She unwrapped the sarong from around her body. Eric's eyes widened, and she smiled. She had gotten the reaction that she was looking for. Tossing the cover-up onto a nearby chair, she slowly stepped into the pool.

He grinned after she did, and she knew it was because of the blissful look on her face. The water felt great. She continued into the water until she stood in front of him.

"You ready?"

She nodded, and he placed his arms around her waist and started to move backward.

"Wrap your arms around my neck."

She did as he asked, and he lay back. Her arms tightened instinctively.

"Loosen your arms some."

She did as he asked, and he continued moving backward in the water. He had made a few laps before she relaxed completely. The man was a good swimmer. She didn't know how he managed to swim and stay afloat with her practically laying on top of him. He also seemed to be using every muscle he had, and there were plenty of them to use. They swam by Irene and Scott, who waved at them. Eric swam around the pool a few more times before swimming over to the edge. Standing up, he placed his hands under her arms and lifted her out of the pool. His strength was extraordinary.

"How was that?"

She nodded. It had been very enjoyable, with the exception of when he had first started swimming toward the deep end of the pool. Being in such close proximity to him had been nice. A long moment of silence passed between them. She began to wonder what it would be like to be married to him, to have kids with him. Dividing the holidays up so that they were spent in an even amount of time between their two families. It would definitely be different from what she was currently used to. She knew what her plans were for every holiday without having to think about it.

She sighed and looked away. His hands came up and turned her head until she looked back at him. He sucked in a deep breath at the intense look in her eyes.

"What are you thinking about?"

She shook her head not wanting to share something so personal, so intimate with him so soon. He came closer to her.

"Well, I will tell you what I am thinking about." He moved even closer. "I am thinking about kissing you."

Her eyes widened, and before she could blink, his lips were coming up to meet hers. She leaned forward, and he pulled her back into the pool with him.

His warm tongue slipped into her mouth. She gasped as he lowered them into the water. A second later, she found out why he had. His hand came up and found her breast. All sorts of thoughts started raging through her head.

She had been kissed before but never like this. His kiss was making her world tilt off its axis. That axis quickly righted itself when his hand slipped between her thighs. She lifted her head breaking their kiss.

"What are you doing?" she asked, after she gasped.

He let his hands do the explaining for him, and she gasped again as he pushed her bikini bottom aside and slid his finger inside of her. It was a different sensation for her. She had to bite her lips to keep from crying out as he added a second finger. The feeling it produced in her was overwhelming. She closed her eyes as his mouth came back down on her again. His lips had barely touched her again when someone let out a shrill whistle. Eric took his time releasing her. He was even slower to remove his hand from underneath her bikini bottom, and she really didn't mind.

She should mind because the water didn't hide much, but they were far enough from everyone else that their activities probably hadn't been noticed. A glance around told her that everyone seemed to busy doing their own thing. She looked up to see Arthur standing at the opposite end of the pool.

"I hate to ruin your fun, kids, but the food is ready, and my grandchildren are hungry."

Owen hopped out of the pool and pulled Gaia out behind him. "Dad, I think that I may have more gray hair than you do. I think that I have outgrown being called a kid."

She could tell that it was a slight exaggeration on Gaia's part, but the comment was still funny. Everyone exited the pool and headed for the tent. Within minutes, they were sitting down at the tables eating. The food was good, and Keirra had to force herself not to overeat.

"So Eric tells us that you are a triplet," Irene commented, as she reached for her drink.

She nodded. "It is hard for some people to believe, but it is true."

Gaia picked up the bottle of mustard. "Who is the oldest?"

Keirra laughed at the question. "My sister Kayla by three minutes. It seems that I didn't want to come out first, and I wasn't too anxious about coming out second, but I had to. Kristen was behind me pushing."

There were a few chuckles around the table.

"What is it like have two identical sisters?" Marianne asked.

Keirra shrugged. "It is fun being a triplet. I also consider myself lucky because I was born with two best friends. Now don't get me wrong. We don't always get along, but we are always there for each other."

"Well, hopefully we will be seeing you again and maybe your sisters as well," Marianne said.

Keirra's gaze flew to Eric, and he smiled and shrugged. He seemed okay with the idea, and that made her a little nervous. A playboy should not be willing to accept anything that was permanent especially when it came to relationships. Maybe he really was trying to reform himself. Half an hour later, the adults were still sitting around the table, and the kids were off playing.

"Anyone have any suggestions on what we should do next?"

"I do, but the kids can't be involved," Owen stated in response to his wife's question, and it earned him an elbow in the ribs.

Gaia gave Owen a pointed look. "That is how we got those three in case you forgot."

Owen wiggled his eyebrows suggestively. "Yes, but we fixed that, didn't we?"

Marianne interrupted before Gaia had the chance to reply. "I say it's time that Mom opens her presents."

Eric stood seconding the suggestion. It took a few minutes to put the leftovers up and to gather the kids up, but moments later they were all sitting in the living room. She was surprised that people living in such a beautiful home would walk around in their swimsuits as if it were an everyday norm. She could see why Eric was such a well-rounded person. She gasped as he physically picked her up and sat her in his lap as if she weighed absolutely nothing.

"What are you doing?"

"Giving Irene a place to sit so Mom can have the recliner. Keirra looked up and realized he was telling the truth. She had been so caught up in her thoughts that she hadn't realized they had run out of room.

Scooting back a little, she settled herself in his lap. If her sisters could see her now, they would be rolling over each other laughing. Eric's persuasion had her doing things that she normally wouldn't do. He was definitely starting to make her rethink her ideas and opinions of him.

Charlotte seemed to be enjoying herself quite a bit. She had already opened Eric's gift. He had bought her a beautiful blouse she had been fawning over but had yet to buy. Keirra was a little surprised a man who told her he didn't like to shop was able to pick out such a nice gift. Keirra tried to clear her mind and focus on the presents Eric's mother was opening. If her mother were alive, she would be four years younger than Charlotte. Sometimes she believed that her mother had just stayed around until she was sure that her daughters were okay. Then again who really knew. Aneurysms were so unpredictable that it was hard to say. Her mother had been a strong woman, but Keirra was still smart enough to realize that her mother and father had had a relationship that was rare. The term *soul mates* always came to mind when she thought of her parents.

She turned and looked back at Eric wondering if she would ever feel that way about him. At first glance, she thought that they were exact opposites, but they seemed to be more alike when she really thought about it. He pushed her beyond her reservations, and he did it so effectively that it was starting to become a little scary. She smiled because this was going to be a very interesting development. "What has you smiling?"

Keirra almost jumped off his lap, and he chuckled. "I didn't mean to frighten you."

She shook her head. This time, it was her fault. She should be paying attention to the presents that were being opened. After all, it was a birthday party.

"I will tell you later."

She really did turn her attention back to Charlotte who was opening her last present. It was a cream-colored cashmere sweater. The sweater must have been something that she had wanted as well judging about her reaction. Charlotte thanked everyone for her gifts before everyone pitched in and helped to clean up the living room.

Gaia rubbed her hands together in anticipation. "It is time for cake and ice cream."

Keirra felt her stomach grumble and groaned. There was no way she should be hungry considering the amount of food she had just consumed. But if there was one thing she had, it was a weakness for ice cream. Especially Ben and Jerry's. There were always at least three containers in the freezer in the event of an emergency.

Everyone headed back outside, and she followed. She gasped as she was pulled into a corner without warning. When she realized it was Eric, she relaxed but not before hitting him in the chest.

"You just insist on scaring the hell out of me, don't you?"

He pulled her close to him. "It isn't intentional. I promise, and it does seem that you are the one who is always daydreaming."

She dropped her forehead onto his shoulder. He had a point there. His hand came down and lifted her chin up.

"Besides I pulled you back here for a reason."

Before she could ask what that reason was, his lips came down on hers. His talented tongue slid into her mouth, and she melted against him. The man made her knees weak with his kisses.

"Yeah, Mom, they are still in here, and they are making out."

Their kiss ended abruptly because Keirra jumped. Eric growled before saying something in Spanish that sounded really close to a profanity from the little Spanish she did know. She watched him turn to look at his sister and could see Marianne's smiling face over his shoulder.

"Yes, we are, and do you mind?"

Marianne shook her head. "No, but Mom does. She is ready to cut the cake."

Eric groaned again before turning back to Keirra. He gave her an apologetic look and placed a quick kiss on her lips before stepping back.

"We will finish this later."

She allowed Eric to take her hand and lead her outside. She could tell that he had hoped to sneak away a little longer, but that hadn't gone as planned. Not that she would have minded. Still he seemed to take it all in stride.

Then again he didn't expect anything else from her nor her from him. She knew that he gave as good as he got. It had been a good idea to come to Atlanta to meet his family. She learned a lot about him. More than she ever thought she would. More than she ever realized that she wanted to, and there was so much more left to discover, and she planned to discover it all.

Chapter Eight

Kayla muttered to herself as she rushed out of the house. She was late, and she hated being late for anything even if it was just a lunch date between her and Jonah. She always prided herself on her punctuality. A wardrobe malfunction was what caused her to be later. She had chosen a blouse that had a big stain on it. It had gone unnoticed until she had put it on. She had no idea how the stain had gotten there. She had quickly replaced her soiled blouse and jeans with a Delft blue knee-length silk sheath dress.

The only thing that made her feel better about the situation was that blue was her favorite color. It also didn't hurt that the color looked good on her. She made it to her car and made her way to Sam's Café as quickly as she could without breaking the speed limit. The last thing she needed was a speeding ticket especially one issued to her by her sister's boyfriend. She was fortunate enough to find a parking spot directly in front of the restaurant.

Shutting off the engine, she reached over and grabbed her purse before getting out of her car. She closed the door and ran straight into a solid wall. The first thing she noticed was the wall smelled incredibly good. The second thing she noticed was the wall had nice hands. Or rather a nice hand since the other was preoccupied with trying not to spill the contents his bag held.

When she was able to right herself she went to apologize, but the apology struck in her throat once she got a direct look at the wall she had run into. She had run into James Denton or better known as Mike on *Desperate Housewives*. Okay, she was exaggerating slightly. This guy could only be considered a look alike. Although he was tall and ruggedly built with thick wavy black hair that begged for her to run her fingers through it. His green shirt swathed a massive chest, and the well-worn jeans that covered a well-structured butt almost took her breath away as reached to pick up a small bag that he hadn't managed to save.

Smooth, lightly tanned skin accentuated by straight white teeth, but it was his eyes that captivated her. He had an angular face with expressive light green eyes she could get lost in. She studied his sharp features, high cheekbones, a straight nose, stubborn jaw and full lips. He had a mustache that connected to a goatee, and both were neatly trimmed. When she realized she was near drooling, she pulled back, and this time she was able to get an apology out along with a small smile. She had to admit she wasn't as embarrassed when she realized he was studying her with as much interest as she had for him.

"Excuse me. I usually don't have a habit of not looking where I am going."

He flashed her a grin that made time stop or at least slow down. "That is okay. It was as much my fault as it was yours."

The smooth baritone of his voice made her knees knock before she could stiffen them. He smiled again, and the effect was worse. She cleared her throat to keep herself from jumping on the man and dragging him into her car so she could have her way with him.

"I didn't realize people in Baxley moved so fast."

The reference made her frown slightly. He made it seem like he was familiar with Baxley, and she knew for a fact she had never seen him before. She would have remembered him. He also didn't seem to know who she was, confirming her assumption.

She gave him another smile. "They normally don't, but I'm not from Baxley, so I don't fall under that criteria."

He laughed. "Well I am from Baxley, but I have been gone a long time."

That statement made her eyebrows rise. "Oh really? Well, if you don't mind, may I ask who you are?"

Once again his lips curved upward. The sexy stranger held out his hand. "Excuse me. I must have been out of Baxley too long since my manners seemed to have escaped me."

Kayla held out her hand and let him engulf it with his larger one.

"My name is James Feldon. I am Dennis Feldman's son."

Kayla really did lose all capability of speech after that statement. She was standing in front of Dennis Feldon's son, and she was drooling over him. What was even stranger was that he was drool worthy.

"And you are?"

She knew Mr. Feldon had a son, but they never met him because he was already gone from Baxley by the time she and her sisters arrived. She frowned when she tried to recall recent pictures of him. She couldn't, and she would have remembered if she had. This man was born to be in front of a camera.

She realized that he was speaking, but she hadn't heard any of it. He tilted his head to the side giving her his breathtaking grin again.

"I am asking what your name is."

Kayla could feel herself begin to blush as she smiled. "Sorry. I'm usually a lot more organized than this. I guess I didn't get enough sleep because I'm definitely not with it today."

She watched James breathe a mock sigh of relief. "Good, I was beginning to wonder if you had a concussion from our collision."

Kayla couldn't help the laughter that bubbled up from her throat at his sense of humor. "No. I assure you I am fine, and again I apologize for not paying attention. If anything needs to be replaced, I will pay for it. By the way, my name is Kayla Smith. Ask your father, and he can confirm just how organized I normally am."

He waved the small bag. "You didn't harm anything. I held onto the food. This is just the condiments and plastic silverware, but I will be sure to confirm that with my father."

Kayla laughed. He had a sense of humor, and she liked it. She also liked that he was going to ask his father about her. It should prove to be interesting.

"Well, I hate to seem rude, but I have a lunch date with a good friend that I am extremely late to."

James nodded although he didn't seem to be in that much of a rush to leave either. If he didn't have a bag of food in his hand, and she wasn't meeting Jonah, she would have asked for an impromptu date. Instead, she smiled. "Well, it was nice meeting you."

He bestowed his devastating smile upon her again. "It was nice meeting you as well. Maybe I will see you around some time."

Kayla nodded herself as she stepped away from James.

"I definitely hope so," she murmured before turning and heading into the entrance of Sam's Café.

She spotted Jonah right away and joined him at the booth. As she did, her mind was still on James Feldon. Jonah greeted her with a kiss on the cheek.

"Well, you are fashionably late today, aren't you?"

She made a face as she sat her purse beside her. "I had an involuntary last-minute outfit change, and then I ran into the man I have been looking for all of my life."

Jonah choked on his drink while she picked up the one he had ordered for her. He was such a good friend, yet his expression was comical. She could tell he was trying to comprehend the statement she just made.

"What did you say?"

Kayla grinned. "You heard me right."

She watched as Jonah composed himself before continuing. "I know you aren't referring to me, so who are you referring to?"

"James Feldon, who happens to be Dennis Feldon's son."

Jonah shook his head. "Wait. Hold on a second before you continue. I need time to collect myself."

Kayla sat back with a smile and watched as Jonah physically prepared himself to hear what she had to say. He was such an attorney. The only thing missing was his yellow note pad and pen.

He gave her a serious look. "Okay, I am ready."

Kayla laughed at his expression. "You have already heard everything."

He shook his head. "Well, I need you to repeat that for me because I don't think I heard you correctly."

Kayla shook her head. "Exactly what is it that I am repeating?"

Jonah gave her a pointed look. "The part about you meeting the man you have been looking for all of your life."

Kayla grinned before relaying what had just happened a few moments before. When she finished, the only thing that Jonah could do was laugh.

"Well, I don't know what to say for the exception that I am happy for you, and I hope that it works out."

Kayla sighed. "I hope so too considering he doesn't know he is the one that I have chosen."

Jonah gave her a huge grin. "Kayla, any man who had a brain would know that he was the one when it comes to you. The real question is does James want to be the one."

* * * *

James chuckled as he walked into his father's house. His father appeared around the corner a moment later.

"Where are the kids?"

His dad smiled. "In the backyard checking out your old tree house."

James found himself frowning. That tree house was old. "Is that old thing safe?"

His dad nodded. "I have kept it up over the years. First out of hope that your mother would come back, and after that out of habit."

James didn't reply as he headed to the kitchen with the food from Sam's Café. His parents' bitter divorce was something that still weighed heavily on his mind, especially considering his marriage to Nicole had ended the same way. He would prefer to focus on the good things like Sam's Cafe being exactly how he remembered it, and he couldn't wait to take his children there.

"I had an interesting run in while I was at Sam's Café."

His father gave him an inquisitive look. "You did?"

James chuckled. "I ran into a woman by the name of Kayla Smith."

A smile automatically appeared on his father's face, and he knew she had to be of good character as she'd claimed to be.

"She is one of the women I have been telling you about."

James sat the bags on the counter. "Tell me about her."

His father shook his head. "I guess you were too busy to hear me the first time I told you."

James began to pull the food out of the bags feeling a little insulted by his father's comment. "Dad, you know why that was. I have had a lot on my plate lately."

His father nodded. James was aware that everyone knew of the turmoil in his life. His life hadn't been easy the past several months . . . years.

"Yes, I do, but that doesn't excuse rudeness."

James chuckled under his breath at his father's frankness. It was something he had missed, something that he'd taken for granted at one time, but almost losing him changed that. Receiving the call from the hospital saying his father'd had a heart attack had taken years off his life. Fortunately, his father was okay, but he had a lot of lost time to make up for.

"You are right, and I apologize. I promise it won't happen again. So if you want to tell me about Kayla now, I will listen. I promise."

His father nodded, a slight smile on his face. "Kayla is one of the women that has been checking on me since my heart attack. Her two identical sisters are the other two women."

He looked at his father with surprise. "She is a triplet?"

"An identical triplet."

It only made her more intriguing to him. She was obviously unique in more ways than one. "Is she a nice woman?"

His father's smile was genuine when he responded. "Very nice. She will give you everything she has if you need it. It's the way she has always been."

James paused before continuing with his next question. "Is she single?"

His father shrugged. "I think she is, but I'm not sure. What I can tell you about her is she teaches History at the high school. Her sister Keirra is a math teacher at the middle school, and her other sister Kristen owns a local daycare."

James nodded. That was good information for him to have. It was his first true day back in Baxley, and it had been a busy one. The first trip had been brief to check on his father and make sure he was okay. He'd set up in-home care until he could pack everything in Austin and prepare them for their move to Baxley. His children were excited about the move, and it made him happy. Still, he knew it was going to get a lot busier. The kids had to get enrolled in school, and he wanted to get it done no later than Monday. His children's education was important to him.

"Is there anything else I should know about Kayla?"

His father nodded. "She is a good woman, and if you hurt her, a lot of people will come after you, including myself."

James sighed. He didn't take his father's threat lightly. He wasn't bothered by it either because he had no intention of getting involved with anyone anytime soon.

Chapter Nine

Keirra opened her eyes as the sunlight hit them and the aroma of bacon found her nose. Her stomach grumbled. There were two things that could wake her. One was the smell of coffee, and the other the smell of bacon. She smiled to herself as she rolled over onto her back. It had been a very interesting weekend. Once everyone had gone, Charlotte and Arthur had retired upstairs, and it had only been Eric and her left, but she hadn't lasted long. She fell asleep on him, and he had carried her to her room and tucked her in.

The only reason she was awake now was because of the aroma of the bacon. The food she consumed yesterday was gone, and she was starving. After getting out of bed, she freshened up and headed for the kitchen.

She was shocked to find Eric and Arthur in the kitchen doing the cooking. Eric had turned and looked at her when he heard her enter the kitchen. She instantly began to wonder if this was what it would be like to wake up to Eric every morning. A man that could cook was a turn-on. She didn't find it appealing to have to be the one to do all of the cooking in the relationship. The smell of coffee drifted over to her, and she looked at the pot with longing before entering the kitchen. Both men greeted her, and Eric instructed her to have a seat. A moment later he brought her a cup of coffee. She took a grateful sip of the black coffee, turning down the cream and sugar he offered. It was the only way she could drink it.

She wasn't certain when she had become addicted to the stuff, but she had to have one cup every morning. Her eyes closed, and she murmured an appreciative thank-you to him.

Several minutes later, Charlotte appeared in the kitchen, and she greeted everyone before taking a seat at the table with Keirra. The way that Charlotte took her seat told her that the men cooked often. Arthur appeared by his wife's side a moment later with a cup of coffee and received a warm kiss for the effort.

She looked at Eric over her cup and wondered what was in store for her. Would he ever greet her the same way? Charlotte pulled her from her thoughts when she spoke.

"I hope you had a good time."

She gave Charlotte a heartfelt smile. "I did. Thank you for making me feel so welcome."

Charlotte reached out and patted her hand. "You are welcome here anytime."

Keirra appreciated Charlotte being such a gracious host. "With a family like yours, it is no wonder that Eric's girlfriends don't want to let him go."

Charlotte gave her a look of surprise and shook her head. "Oh no, dear. You are the first girlfriend that he has brought home."

Keirra's eyes widened, and she managed to get the sip of coffee that she'd taken down without choking. That had been the last thing that she had expected to hear. It was becoming harder and harder to cast him as the bad guy that she needed him to be in order to resist him. She looked at Charlotte, searching for any hint of playfulness on the older woman's face. There was none. Charlotte was completely serious. She looked over at Eric, and as if he felt her eyes on him, he looked over at her. He winked, and she gave him a small smile before looking down at the coffee trying to digest that information.

After breakfast Eric had taken her on the tour of the house as he promised to do earlier. The house had a lot of good memories in it. She could tell by the pictures on the wall and the stories that he told. After the tour they ate a light lunch, and then they began to pack up for the trip back to Baxley. She made no mention of Charlotte's statement, although she was certain that Eric had heard his mother's statement as well. If Eric wanted to talk about it, she would listen, but she wasn't going to be the one to bring it up. To know that she was the only woman that he had brought home to meet his family was humbling. It was also frightening to know that he thought that much of her.

She fell asleep during the car trip back with that thought on her mind. Eric awakened her after he pulled up in front of her house. With a quick kiss, she told him that she would talk to him later and made her way up the walkway. She could feel his eyes on her as she walked toward the house. Once she had the front door open she turned and waved. He returned the wave with a grin before backing out of the driveway and heading home. Keirra closed the door and dropped her bags before sinking to the floor. Eric had her right where he wanted, her and she was certain he knew it.

She took a deep breath before realizing the television was on. Standing up quickly she tried to clear her mind. The last thing she needed was for Kayla to sense something was amiss. She picked up her bags and walked into the living and saw Kayla sitting on the couch. She walked over and collapsed on the couch beside her sister. She couldn't wait to tell her sister about it but only the parts she wanted to reveal.

Kayla grinned at her. "So how was your weekend?"

Keirra fought a smile, but her lips twitched, and she gave in. She relayed all of the details of what had happened over the weekend to Kayla who laughed.

"So are you ready to pay up on our bet yet?"

Keirra shook her head. "We never bet anything."

Kayla snapped her fingers. "I knew I had forgotten something."

Keirra looked at her sister and rolled her eyes. "You have some serious issues."

Kayla laughed and shrugged her shoulders. "We all do."

Keirra sat up as she looked over at her sister. "So did anything exciting happen here while I was gone?"

Kayla nodded. "James Denton moved into town."

Keirra sat up straight. She loved James Denton. Her sisters did as well. They never missed an episode of *Desperate Housewives*.

"Excuse me?"

Kayla smiled. "Actually his look alike did."

Keirra held up her hands. She was completely lost. "Okay, you need to start from the beginning."

Kayla did so and happily. Mr. Feldon was the retired principal of Baxley High School. She knew that Dennis had a son, but she didn't know him because they had never met him. By the time they had moved to Baxley, James was living with Mr. Feldon's ex-wife in another state. Basically she knew nothing of him except he had her sister drooling.

A smile came to her face. "So there is a chance you will fall head over heels in love before I do?"

Kayla laughed. "Are you kidding? I am already in love."

Keirra shook her head and stood up. It was irrational that her sister was willing to admit she was in love with a man she hardly knew, and Kayla was never irrational. Still if her sister could become irrational over such a thing, Keirra knew there was no hope for her.

It was getting late, and there were some things that she needed to prepare for tomorrow. She had a feeling that it was going to be an interesting week.

* * * *

Keirra sighed as she sat down at the table joining her sisters at Sam's Café. It was their weekly hangout during the week. She appreciated it even more now that Kristen wasn't living with them anymore.

Keirra looked over at Kristen who was glowing. With her sister looking so happy, she couldn't be upset that things were no longer the same. She also noticed her sister looked so content with the way that things were. It was mainly due to Randy. She had her own sense of contentment, and as much as she didn't want to admit it, Eric was the reason behind that.

They talked on the phone last night before she had gone to bed, and half of her night had been spent dreaming of him. Even now he was dominating her thoughts. She rotated her head from side to side to clear it.

"So was anyone's day as interesting as mine?"

Both sisters groaned in reply, and Kristen sighed before she spoke. "Yes, but let us share good news first, if there is any."

Kayla spoke first. "Jamie Feldon was enrolled into my class today."

Keirra laughed. "Jana Feldon was enrolled into my class."

Kristen joined Keirra. "Jenna and Josh Feldon were enrolled into my day care today."

Kayla's mouth dropped open in shock at the major revelation. "He has four kids?"

Keirra nodded, trying to keep her own shock at bay. A man with four children would be a challenge, but her perfectionist sister would find a way to manage.

"Seems like it," Keirra murmured.

Kristen sighed. "I hate to spread gossip, but Zebbie said that he moved back here to help Mr. Feldon recover as well as himself."

Kayla's eyebrows rose. "From?"

Kristen's expression was full of sympathy. "His wife died in a car wreck about six months ago."

"Oh, that is *awful*," Kayla exclaimed.

Keirra couldn't agree more. It was awful. No one should have to experience a tragedy like that. They all knew it first hand. Nadia came up to the table and took their orders. Once she left the table, all eyes fell on Keirra. She held her hands up in surrender since she knew what was coming.

"I had a good time. Can we just leave it at that?"

"No," Kayla and Kristen replied simultaneously.

She sighed as Kayla proceeded to fill Kristen in on Keirra's weekend. By the time Kayla was finished, Kristen sat there smiling. Her gaze turned to

Keirra.

"See, I told you Eric wasn't a bad guy."

Keirra rolled her eyes. "I never said he was."

And she hadn't. She just thought of him as a bad guy for her. His reputation was a little disconcerting to her at times. Their food arrived saving her from any more torture until she had a full stomach. Maybe then she could think. They all began to dig into their food. Most of their food was gone before anyone spoke again, and it was Kristen who did so first.

"Before I forget, I want to invite you guys over to the house for dinner sometime this week."

Keirra thought that it was sweet that Kristen wanted to invite her sisters over to her place for Thanksgiving. This was going to be the first holiday that they had spent apart in their entire lives otherwise. Hopefully Kristen would stop worrying about them so much and concentrate on herself. Even as she thought it, she knew it would never happen. Kristen was very maternal even though she was the youngest, and she knew her sister always would be. Still she was very happy Kristen and Randy had been able to overcome their past to step forward together to the future.

A smile came to her face as she thought about Eric. As much as she didn't want to admit it, she was starting to think Eric was the man she needed in her life. He was good for her because he challenged her. She needed to be challenged. She thrived on challenges. Eric would also keep her grounded when she was out of control. Most importantly, he would test her need to be in control. So far, he was definitely doing a good job of it. She looked over at Kristen, who was deep in thought. Maybe her sister's thoughts would get her mind off Eric.

"What is on your mind?"

Kristen grinned. "Eric."

Keirra's eyebrows rose. "I may be a little new to this, but isn't that where my thoughts should be?"

Kayla gave her sister a teasing glance. "Are they?"

Keirra gave Kayla a look full of impatience. "No more than you are supposed to be thinking about James Feldon."

Kayla winked. "You won't get an argument here."

Kristen shook her head at the two of them. "Some things never change."

Kayla laughed, and Kristen took one last bite of her honey mustard chicken and pushed the plate away. Keirra ate the green beans that she had left behind on her plate. A few minutes later, Kayla pushed her plate away.

"So what do you two have planned for the rest of the week?" Kristen asked before taking a sip of soda.

Kayla shrugged. "Nothing out of the ordinary."

Keirra nodded. "Same here. Why do you ask?"

Kristen grinned. "I was thinking of spaghetti night on Wednesday for dinner if you guys can come over to the house."

Keirra rubbed her stomach in anticipation. That sounded good, and they hadn't had spaghetti since Kristen had moved out. It wasn't that they couldn't cook it themselves. It was that Kristen made the best spaghetti.

Keirra could already taste it. "That sounds good."

Kristen graced her with her scheming smile, and Keirra began to have a sinking feeling.

"Good, but there is one condition."

Keirra could feel her stomach begin to tighten in anxiety. Whenever Kristen's issued stipulations it was never a good thing. "What is the condition?"

Kristen's smile grew. "You have to invite Eric."

Keirra closed her eyes and groaned. She might have dropped her head on the table, but it would have caused too much racket. One of these days she was certain her sisters were going to kill her or make her an emotional wreck, if not both.

Chapter Ten

"Will you stop that," Keirra snapped at Eric under her breath.

He had been doing his best to irritate her all night. Her best guess was that her sisters had put him up to it, but she had no way of proving it. She was starting to get pissed off because he was making it hard for her to enjoy her sister's spaghetti. He looked over at her with the innocence of a two-year-old.

"What?"

She started to tell him exactly what to stop doing, but she remembered other people where at the table with them, and they would only be amused by the situation. Maybe this was her fault because she had chosen the wrong outfit to wear. She had thought the ivory print tank dress would be safe. Sure, it was a little form fitting, but it was knee length at least until she sat down, and Eric was taking advantage of the length.

"Are you always this beautiful?"

She looked at him as though he'd lost his mind. Actually, she was pretty certain that he had. He whispered the comment, but evidently, Kayla had heard him because she snickered. Keirra groaned and dropped her face into her hands. Eric smiled. She didn't want to admit he made her feel beautiful. She was an attractive woman and heard the words quite often but not from men that meant it. At least not from someone who meant it simply because it was how he felt, not because he was trying to talk her into bed. Not that she would mind being in his bed. She paused when she realized where her thoughts were going. She might need to have her head examined. Looking over at him, she realized that he was watching her expectantly. His confidence could be maddening at times.

"You haven't seen me in the morning," she grumbled.

He smiled wickedly. "Is that an invitation?"

She gave him an appalled look that he would even make such a suggestion.

Then again, she shouldn't be surprised considering he was a man, a virile man. He didn't need any encouragement.

"Absolutely not."

Eric laughed as his hand continued on its journey up her thigh. Fighting off a tremble, she reached for her fork. His hand slid between her thighs, and she clenched them trying to prevent him access. She almost gasped as he tightened his grip on her thigh.

He leaned over to her and whispered into her ear. "You have very soft skin."

He said something else in Spanish, but it was so sensual sounding that her thighs opened slightly in response, and as in involuntary as the movement was, it gave him the access that he needed. She stood up abruptly, almost knocking the chair over in her haste, and excused herself, quickly flushing in embarrassment at the surprised looks that she received before, rushing for the bathroom.

Once she made it there, she locked the door. One look in the mirror made her wince. Her skin was reddened. After turning on the cold water, she splashed her face and patted it dry. The results were a lot better. She jumped as someone knocked on the door.

"Keirra, are you okay?"

She sighed in relief when she realized that it was Kristen. Her relief grew when she opened the door and saw Kayla there as well. She pulled them both inside the bathroom, closed the door, and locked it once more.

Kristen frowned. "What is wrong with you?"

Keirra looked at her sisters in shock. "Eric was feeling me up under the table."

Seconds later, Kayla and Kristen fell over each other in laughter. She narrowed her eyes, and her sisters tried not to laugh as hard but failed miserably.

Keirra folded her arms over her chest. "I should have known you two would find this funny."

They held their hands up as they tried to straighten their faces and control their laughter.

"I'm sorry, but if you could see your face right now." Kayla gasped.

"I can," she muttered through clenched teeth.

Her sour expression was fitting considering the circumstances. After walking over to the commode, she sat down and crossed her legs. She knew it had been a bad idea to invite Eric, but her sister has insisted, and now she was locked in the bathroom with her sisters. Could it truly get any worse than this?

Kristen came forward first. "Come on, Keirra. You act like it is a crime to share physical contact with a person that you are attracted to."

Keirra almost pouted. "I'm not attracted to Eric."

"Are you certain? Those gorgeous brown eyes; silky black hair; straight teeth, nice, firm butt—"

"*Hey!*"

Kayla smiled knowingly, and Keirra realized that her older sister loved that she had the ability to get her riled up.

"Just trying to make sure you take a good look at what you have in front of you."

She rolled her eyes. "You guys are awful to make fun of me like this."

Kristen patted her shoulder. "Cheer up. No one ever said it was easy falling in love, but it sure is fun for those watching."

Keirra looked at her sister and wondered if she had lost her mind. "That is the most idiotic thing I have ever heard. Just in case you didn't know, the whole process is supposed to be fun for everyone if it is going to count."

Kristen stood over her with her arms crossed. "How would you know that?"

Keirra had to keep from cursing when she realized that she'd been had again. There was no way she could pretend to be an expert at love. She gave her sisters an evil look and received a smile from both of them in return. It was times like these when she wouldn't mind been a single child.

"You like him, and when you admit it things will be a lot easier."

With that said, Kristen turned and left the bathroom with Kayla following her. It took Keirra a few minutes to compose herself.

How dare Kristen insinuate that she liked Eric more than what she was letting on. Even if it was true to a certain degree, she didn't want it broadcasted to the entire world. Liking Eric more than she already did could be dangerous. Falling for an officer of the law broke her number one rule. She might be willing to take the risk of getting to know Eric, but falling in love with him was something that she wouldn't do, something that she couldn't allow herself to do.

Taking a deep breath, she exited the bathroom. She headed back to the kitchen and took her seat making sure to move her chair a good foot away from Eric for good measure. When she resumed eating, she was thankful for the ability to eat in peace for the rest of the meal. Unfortunately, when the meal was over, Keirra remembered that she would have to take Eric home. She didn't know why she let her sisters bait her into doing things she knew could backfire.

Right now, she just wanted to get Eric to his home and get to her own so that she could get in bed. She was tired after tonight's events. They left the house right behind Kayla.

"See you at the house," Kayla called out the window as she drove off.

Keirra got inside of her own car and started the ignition while waiting for Eric to get in. As soon as he had, she backed out of the driveway. After driving a block, she hit him in the arm then resumed driving.

"That was for your behavior tonight."

He chuckled. "I thought that I handled myself pretty well."

"You would," she grumbled. She really had been shocked by his behavior. The last thing she had expected from Eric was for him to grope her under the dinner table. A kiss maybe, but feeling her up, no. She pulled up in front of Eric's house, and he looked over at her.

"Will you come inside for a minute?"

Her eyes widened in surprise. "You can't be serious."

He chuckled. "I have something that I want to show you."

She shook her head. If he thought that she was going to fall for that line, he was in for a surprise. She crossed her arms over her chest. "I am sure that you do."

He held his hand up in Scout's honor. "Irene sent some pictures from Saturday to me by e-mail, and I printed them out."

She sighed heavily knowing that she should head home, but she really did want to see the photos. If this was a trick, he was going to pay. She turned off the engine and stepped out of her car. He led the way up the walkway. As soon as she stepped inside, she smiled. His house was very nice. It was also very Eric. The house spoke of warmth and the sense of wanting to come in and relax.

"I will be back in a second."

He left the room, and she did a slow circle taking everything in as she went. A second later Eric returned. Maybe he had been telling the truth because he had a package of photos he handed to her. She took a seat on the sofa and opened the package. The photos were nice. What amazed her was she did fit in with his family.

She had a genuine smile on her face in every picture, and she was also by a member of the Brooks family in each photo telling her how much she really fit into the family. Something she never thought she would see . . . feel. The next thing she noticed was the last of the pictures seemed to be of just her and Eric. They looked really good together. It surprised her to see the happiness on her face was authentic. It was a little frightening. What scared her a little more was he was staring at her intensely in a few of the pictures. It was easy for her to interpret his look. He wanted her, and he cared for her, and it was evident in the pictures. She placed them back in the package. As much as she fought pursuing anything with him, she knew she hadn't made a mistake.

"If you want copies let me know," he stated as he took the photos back.

She nodded. "Yes, I would."

She stood up and handed the photos back to him. "Thank you for showing those to me."

"You are welcome."

It was getting late, and she needed to get home and get ready for work. She headed for the front door. He followed close behind her. She stepped aside as he reached for the door, and opened it.

"Thank you for inviting me tonight. I had a good time."

"I am glad you did."

She knew as soon as the words were out of her mouth that she meant them, and when she looked up, she also knew he was going to kiss her. Eric proved her right when he stepped closer to her. His lips came down on hers, and her eyes drifted closed, but the kiss ended before she expected it to. The amount of desire in his eyes was somewhat frightening.

"I want to take this to the next level. I want to make love to you," he whispered, his voice raspy with need.

Her mouth dropped open, and she couldn't close it to save her life. That had been the last thing she had expected to hear from Eric. Shock kept her from protesting as his mouth covered hers again, and the kiss seemed to go on forever until she ended the kiss. She came to her senses and put a little space in between them. Confused didn't begin to describe how she felt. She knew she needed to think this through, and this was neither the time nor the place. If she took this step with him, there was no going back. She wouldn't be able to keep the emotions she hid at bay, could no longer hide how much she wanted him. She needed to think about this, but there was no way she would be able to think rationally with him in such close proximity. His effect on her could only be described as intoxicating.

She brought her hands up to his chest, but instead of pushing him away like she should, she just rested them there.

"I don't think we should do this."

He brought his hands up to cover hers. "Why not?"

She gave him the best excuse she could think of at the time, even though it was a lousy one. "We haven't known each other long enough."

He searched her expression. "Do you really feel that way?"

When she didn't answer, he let go of her hands and opened the front door wider to give her room to escape. For some reason unknown to her, at least consciously, she didn't take the escape route. Instead, she closed her eyes briefly and took a deep breath before reopening them. He stood there, giving her a way out, and she knew she should take it. Instead, she pushed the door closed and fumbled until she found the lock.

Eric took over for her, making sure his door was locked before sweeping her up into his arms as if she weighed nothing. He carried her down the hall to his room. When they made it to his room, he set her on her feet. He made quick work of their clothes making her wonder if she had what it took to satisfy Eric. She had a nice body, and she was sure of it because she did aerobics with Billy Blanks three mornings out of the week. Yet, she still felt nervous. She would find out soon enough.

Before she could blink, they were on the bed, and he was over her. His attention fell to her breasts. She definitely had enough to please. Instead of going straight for her breasts, he shocked her by bringing his lips down on hers. Another shock came when his hands slid between them and found her hot and moist like he had at the dinner table. This time there was no underwear in the way. A gasp escaped her as he began to increase feelings that she wasn't familiar with. Desire surged through her, and she clutched at his shoulders.

The pleasure became unbearable, and her hips began to move on their own accord. Her release followed shortly afterward, and she made sounds that would embarrass her later. She was breathing heavily when he moved away from her. Just as she was getting ready to protest, she heard the rattle of a foil packet and knew that he was protecting them. She was thankful for that, and when he came back over her, she smiled. He began to enter her. It felt different from anything she had ever experienced before. She moaned as the pleasure began to build up in her once more. The moan turned into a gasp as Eric slid completely into her. There was brief discomfort, but it was gone before it really registered. He held still and made sure that she was okay before moving again. She tightened around him instinctively, and he gritted his teeth to hold himself in check.

He didn't have to worry about his control or lack of for long. A few deep strokes later, she climaxed again on a sharp cry of pleasure. The feel of her body rhythmically tightening and relaxing around him pulled him over the edge with her. He whispered her name, and the emotion behind it made her shiver. She was grateful when he summoned enough strength to move to the side instead of crushing her with his weight. His arms went around her, and she marveled at how good it felt to have them around her. Her joy faded a little as she thought about what she would have to do to stay there.

Chapter Eleven

Keirra shifted in her sleep then went still as she brushed into something hairy and solid. Her eyes popped open, and she groaned silently at the soreness she felt. She'd thought last night was a dream. Now that she realized it hadn't been, she could feel her heart rate speed up. Had she done something she now regretted? Well if she did, she wasn't going to have time to think about it because Eric chose that moment to open his eyes. He smiled as his gaze met hers.

"Good morning."

"Good morning," she mumbled.

Not thinking, she made the mistake of sitting up. Realizing she was naked, she quickly pulled the covers up over her, even though she knew it was a foolish notion. The man had seen her body already—all of it. Her cheeks heated at the thoughts of what he had done to her naked body.

His hand came up and touched her arm. "Are you okay?"

She dropped her face into her hands and shook her head. Her thoughts were racing in several directions. It was mostly confusion. Was she moving too fast? Should she have taken the emotional risk she had by sleeping with Eric? She already knew the answer to the question before she finished it. Getting involved with an officer went against everything that she wanted, but anything that was going to be said was interrupted by the phone ringing. She watched his muscles ripple as he performed the simple task of reaching for the phone. He spoke into the receiver, chuckled, and looked at her.

"Yes, she is."

She closed her eyes in horror knowing it was one of her sisters, and worse yet they knew she had spent the entire night with Eric. There was no way she was going to live this down anytime soon. He laughed bringing her back to the current dilemma at hand. How could she get out of bed in the least confrontational way?

"Okay. I will."

When he hung up the phone, he was still grinning. "That was Kayla making sure you were up."

Keirra closed her eyes and groaned. Things couldn't get any worse than this.

"She told me to make sure I send you off with a smile."

She had been wrong about things not getting worse than they already were. Shaking her head, she swung her legs over the bed. She went to get out of the bed, and Eric reached out and grabbed her.

"Where are you going?"

"I have to get home so I can get ready for work."

He pulled her back into the bed with him. "Not before I send you off properly."

She shook her head and rolled her eyes. "You will learn not to take Kayla so seriously."

He smiled wickedly. "But I want to."

Before she could respond, his mouth came down on hers. She was starting to dislike his kisses. They were distracting. Even so, she noticed when he slid his hand between her thighs. She closed her eyes hating that her body responded to him even when she didn't want it to. His mouth left hers, and he moved on to place kisses on her neck. A moan of pleasure sounded from her lips as he continued downward and found her breast. The man knew how to lavish on and worship a woman's body. He took his time, seeming determined to push her to the edge, whether she wanted to go or not. She stiffened as he slid lower. *He isn't going to go there.* Eric slid lower, and she knew he was.

She had half a mind to stop him, but she wanted to experience what he was offering. Her legs still tensed when he lifted them over his shoulders. She cried out as she felt Eric's lips touch her in a way that no one ever had. She reached out her hand and clutched at the bedspread. A scream erupted from her throat when his tongue found the direct link to her release. She couldn't catch her breath because of the sensation flowing through her body. It was too much, and another scream bubbled up from a deep part in her throat as she reached the pinnacle of her release. Instead of stopping, he increased the amount of pleasure that he was giving to her. Her toes curled, and she dug her feet into his shoulders as he pushed her higher. Before she could catch her breath, he came up over her.

He reached for protection and covered himself with it before sliding deep inside of her. Neither of them could take their next breath. She cried out in what was a mixture of pleasure and pain. Another release sneaked up on her, and she experienced a fourth one before Eric let himself find his own release. She barely had time to recuperate before he was pushing her out of bed and out of his front door so she could get to work on time. The short drive home gave her enough time to reflect on everything she didn't want to. The main thing being that Eric was better than a cup of coffee any day.

* * * *

Keirra looked up as Kayla opened the door. "You will never guess who just showed up."

Keirra groaned and closed her eyes. She didn't care who it was. She wasn't up for company. Her only plan was to rest to try to get rid of or ease her stomach cramps so that she wouldn't have to cancel on her sisters this evening. Kayla wanted to have dinner again, so they were going over to join her and Randy again.

"I don't want to know."

"Too bad."

Keirra closed her eyes and tried not to curse at the sound of his voice. This was the last thing that she needed. Opening her eyes, she fought a grimace as Eric came into her view. Even though he was an unwelcome sight, he was still a pleasant one to look at.

Kayla being the traitor that she was backed out of the room closing the door behind her. Keirra sat up slowly but still winced.

Eric noticed and frowned. "What's wrong?"

She looked at him with surprise before smiling. He wanted to know what was wrong with her. Well she was more than willing to tell him. Maybe he would leave her alone.

"It is that time of the month."

His mouth formed the cutest shape of an O she had ever seen.

"Are you okay?"

She would have laughed, but it would hurt too much. The expressions coming and going across his face were very comical.

"Can I do anything to help?"

She nodded her head. "You could leave and let me go back to resting."

He gave her a look, and she sighed knowing what it meant. He wasn't going anywhere. It was too close to dinnertime. Somehow, he'd managed to finagle an invite to dinner. It was the first time they'd been alone together since they had sex. She knew now she couldn't trust herself around him and wanted to avoid that at all costs.

"I have taken some pain medication, but if you have anything stronger, I will take it."

He laughed. "Do you trust me?"

Her eyes narrowed. "Too late to ask that, don't you think?"

"I will take that as a yes. Lie on your back."

She rolled her eyes in exasperation. "Now isn't the time."

He chuckled. "Get your mind out of the gutter."

Instead of replying, she lay back because she didn't think she could sit up any longer without becoming nauseated. Eric came over to the bed. A groan of pain escaped her as Eric's hand pressed into her stomach. He began to massage her achy body, and after a moment, the pain began to subside. Moments later, she was actually able to take a breath without wincing. When the last of the tension left Keirra's body, he pulled back.

"Do you feel better now?"

She sighed in relief. "Yes, I do. Thank you."

She started to wonder where he had learned his technique. Her question must have been distinguishable in her eyes since Eric answered her.

"A trick that Gaia taught me."

Keirra scoffed. "Yeah right."

Eric laughed. "That is what I like about you."

"What?"

He placed a brief kiss on her lips. "You frustrate the hell out of me, yet you manage to make me laugh."

She narrowed her eyes. The man was insane. She made sure he knew that was her opinion.

He chuckled. "That may be true, but you are still a major turn-on."

She shook her head at him. "You are strange."

He smiled. "Stranger by the minute."

Keirra shook her head and sat up slowly. Eric's touch had worked, but it didn't mean she should push it. She swung her legs over the edge of the bed. Eric was a lifesaver. She pulled up her pajama pants and tugged down the matching camisole that had risen up. Showing her skin to Eric wasn't too bright of an idea. He already had a hard time keeping his hands off her. She led the way out of her room and headed downstairs. Kayla was sitting on the couch watching *Deja Vu*. She looked up as she heard Keirra and Eric enter the room.

"Are you feeling better?"

She nodded. "Yes, I am."

"Good enough to go over to Randy and Kristen's?"

"Yes."

Kristen was probably working hard to set everything up for this evening. Thanksgiving was right around the corner, and they would all be too busy to get together again for dinner like this before it did. It had just started to dawn on her that there was a possibility they may be spending the holidays apart. She was happy for Kristen and wouldn't do anything to take away from her sister's happiness. She and Keirra would just have to make the best of things.

"What time do you plan on leaving?"

Kayla nodded in the direction of the television. "As soon as this movie goes off."

Keirra just shook her head and headed into the kitchen with Eric following close behind. She went to the refrigerator and poured herself a cup of water.

"So how was your week?"

She laughed before looking at him. "My students think I am possessed."

His eyebrows rose. "You aren't?"

Keirra almost spit out the water she had just taken a drink of. If she could hit him without hurting herself, she would have. "You aren't funny."

He winked at her. "I have been told otherwise."

"If it was your family, they were just lying to make you feel better."

He stepped closer to her. "My family would never lie to me."

She shrugged because she knew that was probably a true statement. He took her glass out of her hand and took a drink before handing it back to her. She tried not to let him know the action affected her. It was a very intimate act.

She sighed. "So what brings you by?"

He smiled. "I came to pick you up."

She knew Kristen and Randy had invited Eric. Since everyone officially considered her and Eric an item, it was a given. Did it bother her? Not as much as it should. She had to face it the man was getting up under her skin, and he was knocking down her defenses quicker than she could put them up. What was she going to do if she found herself in love with the man? If she thought she could get him to give up his occupation, she might have a fighting chance.

She would never forget the eventful night she lost her father. The night her life had changed forever. Although she was aware most of the things that happened to them afterward might not have happened otherwise. They wouldn't have moved to Baxley. The good high school years they had experienced might not have happened. She and her sisters might not be as close as they were. The exciting times they shared had normally been the consequence of something she had done. She had always been the one who wanted to add excitement. So it might be true that good things come out of tragedy. Even so, she still wasn't ready to take actions that could lead her down that road again.

"Well, I am going to go get ready."

He nodded giving her a teasing glance. "Wear something sexy."

Keirra rolled her eyes at his exaggerated wiggling of his eyebrows as she handed him her cup and walked out of the kitchen. The man was something else. As she made her way up the stairs, she had to wonder if Eric was the one for her. Maybe he was someone who had been put in her way to make her face her fears, or maybe she was just thinking too hard. Either way, she planned to enjoy herself this evening, and that was what she was going to do.

Chapter Twelve

"No, Kristen. That would be ridiculous."

Keirra was surprised to hear the words come from her own mouth, but she meant it. She looked over at Kayla and smiled. They were in the middle of enjoying the wonderful dinner Kristen had prepared. Kristen had brought the subject up of what everyone was going to do for Thanksgiving.

Kristen was trying to figure out a way for everyone to spend Thanksgiving with Randy and his family. It was touching that her sister was trying to make sure that no one felt left, out but it wasn't necessary. As much as she loved her sisters, they were three individuals, and they all knew this day would come at some point.

"I agree."

Her baby sister was always putting others before herself. Keirra reached out and took Kristen's hand in hers.

"This is your time. Kayla and I will manage."

Eric cleared his throat. "If it makes you feel better, I'm going to invite Keirra to my parents' place, and since my mother isn't taking no for an answer, her Thanksgiving plans are taken care of."

Keirra's mouth dropped open and would have dragged on the table if Kayla hadn't elbowed her. She was going to kill him in spite of his innocent expression. He knew exactly what he was doing. How could she say no to his invite in front of her siblings? She knew what their reaction would be. Still she opened her mouth to protest, but Kristen spoke before she could.

Kristen grinned. "Good."

She glared at Eric, and he winked at her. She wanted to tell him he hadn't won the battle yet, but she was distracted when Kristen's smile started to fade a little. She knew why that was when she realized that the arrangements still left Kayla out, and she voiced her concern. It seemed as though Eric was willing to fix that problem as well.

"Kayla is welcome to join us in Atlanta. My parents have more than enough room."

Kayla shook her head. "Oh no. I couldn't impose on the two of you."

Keirra wanted to elbow her, but she was too far away. There was always later, especially when Eric looked so smug. Eric leaned back and grinned.

"The more, the merrier. Besides I am hoping you and Keirra will play a few tricks on the family."

Keirra had finally come out of shock and elbowed Eric. "*Absolutely not.* Besides, who says that I am going?"

He shrugged. "Well, it was worth a try, and I could always have my mother call you, so you can explain to her why you aren't."

Her eyes widened at the impact of his statement. He had her exactly where he wanted her, and he knew it. She tried to close her mouth, and after several attempts managed to.

"*Blackmail,* Eric?"

He nodded without shame. "Whatever it takes."

She could have resorted to bodily harm, but then she would have to explain that as well. Kayla laughed, and Keirra glared at her.

Kayla held up her hands in surrender. "What? It isn't my fault that you have met someone who can beat you at your own game."

Randy cleared his throat and made his own offer. "Kayla, you are more than welcome to join us for Thanksgiving."

Kayla laughed. "Well, thanks for inviting me. I think I will stay here and join Randy and Kristen."

"If only my legs were longer," Keirra muttered at her older sister. It didn't make her feel any better when everyone laughed at what she was implying. It made kicking Kayla underneath the table sound even more tempting.

Kristen smiled. "Well, be that as it may, I'm just happy everyone was going to have somewhere to go for the Thanksgiving holiday."

Everyone resumed eating, and the rest of the dinner conversation was light yet filled with humor. Even she couldn't keep from mellowing and enjoying the rest of the meal. After dinner, everyone pitched in to help clean up. Kristen and Randy were caught making out, which didn't seem to bother them at all. Keirra gave Eric a look of warning when he reached for her and chuckled, but she went in the opposite direction.

As they rode back to the house, Keirra smiled to herself. She was happy that Kristen was happy. After the rocky time that she and Randy had when they had begun dating years ago the two of them deserved all of the happiness that they could get. Eric pulled up into the driveway, and Kayla was out of the SUV before he could turn off the engine.

"Does she always move that fast?"

Keirra rolled her eyes. "Only when there is something on the television she wants to watch."

Eric laughed. "Do you mind if I come in for a little while?"

She shook her head. "No."

They got out of his SUV, and she led the way up the walkway. She shivered. The temperature had dropped since they had left Randy and Kristen's.

They stepped inside, and Kayla was indeed sitting in front of the television. It looked like a special on dinosaurs.

"Make yourself at home. I'm going to go upstairs and change into something more comfortable."

Eric nodded and took a seat on the couch. Keirra turned and made her way upstairs. Once she entered her room, she unbuttoned her jeans and sighed. What had she been thinking to wear jeans? She found a pair of pajama pants and put them on. After pulling her sweater over her head, she tossed it aside and pulled on a T-shirt. She was going for comfort. Relief was what she needed right now. She placed the discarded clothes in the hamper before heading back downstairs. Kayla hadn't moved an inch, and it looked as though the show had sucked in Eric's attention.

She took a seat next to Eric. "What did I miss?"

Giving her a brief glance, he shook his head. "Not much."

It wasn't long before Keirra found herself drawn into the show. She enjoyed shows like this. All of her sisters did. The documentaries always seemed to be informative, and she felt that knowledge was power. It was two hours before anyone moved, and that was because the show ended.

"Well, that was interesting."

"Yes, it was."

Eric stretched and followed it with a yawn. "I had better get going."

He stood up and held out his hand pulling her up beside him. "Let me run upstairs and put some shoes on."

She ran upstairs and slipped into her house shoes. When she came back downstairs, Eric was waiting by the door. They stepped outside together, and she shivered at the cool temperature.

"I won't keep you out here long. If we don't talk this week, I will be here the same time Thursday morning."

She stifled a groan. "I will be ready."

He gave her a brief kiss, and she watched as he ran for his SUV and got in.

When he backed out of the driveway, she went back into the house.

"I like him."

Keirra rolled her eyes. If that wasn't stating the obvious, she didn't know what it was.

"Yes, I know you do, and don't think that you are off the hook. I just happen to be exhausted. I am going to go upstairs and watch a little television before I got to bed instead of mauling you like I want to."

Keirra shook her head before turning to make her way up the stairs.

She was truly exhausted. Hopefully by tomorrow she would be rested enough to start the week off right. She entered her room and undressed before walking into her bathroom. She took a quick shower. Once she was dressed for bed she crawled under the covers and turned the television on, and then set the timer knowing that she wasn't going to stay awake long. Within ten minutes the television was watching her.

* * * *

She woke up to her alarm going off. Hitting the Off button, she climbed out of bed and groggily walked downstairs. She prayed Kayla had programmed the coffeemaker last night. As she reached the bottom of the steps, she got the answer to her question. She inhaled appreciatively. After pouring herself a cup, she sat at the kitchen table and drank it slowly. Thankfully it wasn't a workout day. Seconds later, Kayla came into the kitchen. Keirra looked at her sister over her cup and murmured a good morning and thanks for the coffee.

"Would you like some toast and oatmeal?"

"Yes, please."

Kayla occupied herself with fixing breakfast. When she finished they ate, and Keirra headed back upstairs to get ready for work. Kayla left a little earlier than she did, but that was fine. They would meet up at Sam's Café later on tonight since they were going to be too busy on Monday to meet up there. She finally finished getting dressed and made her way back downstairs.

Keirra headed out the door with a smile on her face. Teaching was something she really enjoyed. She pulled up into the parking lot. After gathering her things up, she walked inside the school. She walked to the front office and signed in. She went to her classroom and began to set up. Time flew by, and the bell signaling the end of the day rang before she expected it.

She pulled into an empty space at Sam's Café. Being the first to arrive she chose their regular table by the window. Kayla and Kristen arrived shortly after. Nadia came right over and took their food and drink orders. She returned to the table with their drinks and sat them down before walking away.

Keirra reached for her soda. "How was everyone's day?"

Kristen nodded. "Mine was pretty good in spite the amount of sick children I have on my hands at the daycare."

Kayla sighed heavily. "Mine was okay, but I have a feeling things are going to go downhill."

Keirra looked at their sister with surprise. "Why?"

Kayla shook her head. "I have a few students looking to pick a fight."

Keirra could feel her blood pressure rise. If it was one thing she didn't like, it was a bully. She'd spent most of her life defending people against them.

"What are you going to do about it," Kristen asked, her voice full of concern.

Kristen shook her head with disappointment. "Well, I have already spoken with their parents once about a prior accident, and for a while, it got better. Now it has started to escalate again. My next step is to call a parent-teacher conference."

Keirra looked at her sister in puzzlement. "We just had one when school started back."

Kayla gave her a grim look. "I know, but the parents who needed to show up didn't. Go figure."

Kristen frowned. "I assume it's the same group of girls keeping the trouble going?"

Kayla sighed. "Just like their parent's did when we were growing up. I guess the saying is true. The apple doesn't fall too far from the tree."

Keirra shook her head in disbelief. "Well, I am sure that you will . . . oh my goodness!"

Everyone looked up as Keirra stopped in mid-speech. When they saw she was looking over their shoulders, Kayla and Kristen turned to look.

"Oh my goodness is right," Kristen murmured.

"Yes, it is," Kayla agreed as she eyed the very attractive man who had just walked in with his family. The whole room—at least the female population—seemed to stop, and with reason. James Feldon was sexy as hell.

Keirra couldn't avoid staring at the man who had caught her sister's attention, and it was very obvious as to why that was now. The man was absolutely gorgeous.

"Do you remember Mr. Feldon being so good looking?"

"Eww," Kristen exclaimed. "We are talking about our formal principal. No one should be thinking about his state of attractiveness."

Keirra ignored Kristen's outrage and shook her head before answering

Kayla's question. "He wasn't an unattractive man, but he was nowhere near as good looking as his son is."

Their food was delivered to their table, probably saving them from embarrassment. Keirra was the first to bring up the subject again once Nadia walked off.

"And you say that I am insane because I don't attack Eric with crazed passion every time I see him."

Kayla laughed. "That is different."

Keirra took a bite of her steak and noodles. "How?"

"His daughter is my student now."

Kristen jumped in. "There are several teachers that teach their own children. But if it became a big deal, you could always have her transferred out of your class."

Keirra smiled as she backed up Kristen. "She has you there."

Kayla shook her head. "If you say so."

Keirra laughed. "I know if I had a guy who looked as good as James Feldon does, I would be all over him."

Kristen laughed. "You do. His name is Eric."

Chapter Thirteen

"Where are we going?"

Randy grinned as he looked over at Kristen. He loved her with everything that he had and was glad that he had been given the chance to show her.

"It is a surprise."

Kristen laughed and settled back into the seat as he drove them into town. He pulled up in front of the jewelry store, and Kristen gave him a quick glance, but she didn't say anything. He pulled into an empty space and killed the engine, and then he got out of his truck and went around to assist Kristen out.

"What are we doing here?"

He cleared his throat. "We are here to look at rings."

She gave him a strange look. They hadn't discussed marriage. Not because he didn't want to but because it hadn't come up. Randy led her inside already imaging the rumors that were going to be flying around before the day ended. Not that he cared. As soon as they stepped inside, Nelson greeted them.

"What brings the two of you in?"

Randy smiled in return. "We are looking for an engagement ring."

Kristen's mouth fell open. Nelson smiled at her expression, and Randy continued on like he hadn't stated anything out of the ordinary.

"Well, I have a few rings for you to look at."

Nelson walked down to another display. Randy followed pulling her behind him. Nelson pulled out a few rings, and Randy had her try them on. His hand had never shaken so badly in his life as he handled the delicate jewelry. Some of the rings were beautiful. By the time they left the store, Kristen looked to be in a daze.

"Which one did you like best?"

She looked up at him in shock and blinked several times before she answered him.

"I liked all of them, but the last two the most."

Both of them had been a matching engagement ring and band. He liked those the most too. Randy helped her up into his truck.

"Why didn't you tell me we were coming to look at rings?"

He gave her a hesitant smile. "Because I didn't know what your response would be."

She opened her mouth, but no sound came out. He stared at her for a moment then closed the passenger door. The trip home was a short but silent one. After they stepped inside the house, Kristen stopped Randy.

"Why did you think I would have a bad reaction to talking about marriage?"

Randy sighed. After my relationship with Lila and even our past, I can't help having doubts.

She smiled as she cupped his cheek in her hand. "You know that I love you, right?"

"Just as much as I love you," Randy stated as he pulled Kristen into his arms.

"Even though we haven't really talked about it, I would love to be your wife."

Her words sent a surge of happiness through him. A smile spread across his face, and he swept her up into his arms and carried her up the stairs to the room they shared. When he laid her down on the bed the amount of love that reflected in her eyes made his heart swell. He looked forward to the day she became his wife.

* * * *

"The two of you what?"

Kristen laughed at Kayla's response.

"I was just as shocked as you were," Kristen stated prior to taking a bite of her blackened chicken. She chewed slowly before continuing.

"The good thing is we talked about marriage and having more kids."

Kristen wiggled her eyebrows. "Before and after. We did a little practicing."

Kayla laughed. "Well, I am happy for the two of you."

Kristen smiled at Kayla before giving Keirra a look of puzzlement. "You are quiet today, and you haven't touched a bite of your food. Is everything okay?"

Keirra shrugged her shoulders and pushed her steak around on her plate then put her fork down.

"I don't know. I guess I am just not hungry."

Both of her sisters looked at her as if she were severely ill.

"You aren't hungry? There must be something wrong," Kristen commented.

Kayla gasped. "Are you pregnant?"

Keirra rolled her eyes skyward, surprised that her sister would suggest something so off the wall. "*Get real.* There is no way I could keep that a secret."

Kristen looked at her with concern. "Then what is it?"

Keirra shrugged. The truth was she didn't know where to start with what was bothering her. One thing was she couldn't get her mind off Eric no matter what she did. That disturbed her deeply. She didn't want to fall for him. Right now, their relationship was fun. She liked it that way. Unfortunately, she felt like she was willing herself to do something inevitable. It was only a matter of time before her heart overruled her head and she got in trouble. She looked up as Kristen wrapped an arm around her.

"Whatever it is, it can't be that bad."

Keirra could only laugh. Kristen had no idea how bad it could be, but she gave her sister a slight squeeze anyway.

"Actually, it could be, but I will pretend it isn't."

Kayla sighed heavily. "Well, will you at least tell us what it is? Maybe we can help, but we won't know until you tell us what the issue is."

Keirra sighed heavily trying to prepare herself for the ribbing that she was getting ready to receive.

"I am falling for Eric."

Her sisters were silent for so long she had to check to make sure they had heard her.

Kristen was the first to respond. "I am sure you have come up with a million reasons as to why that is a bad thing, but personally I can't think of one."

Kayla's express was just as puzzled. "Please don't tell me you are still hung up on this cop thing."

Keirra frowned. Actually, the thought hadn't crossed her mind in a while, and that worried her. She found herself shaking her head. "No, it isn't that."

Both of her sisters' jaws dropped. "Then what is bothering you?"

Keirra laughed at Kristen's question. She thought she'd stated the obvious, but clearly she was going to have to spell it out for her sisters.

Kayla gasped. "You are falling in love with him."

She rolled her eyes at her older sister's dramatics. "I wouldn't go that far."

Keirra shrugged. "But I will admit that I am falling for him a little more than I am comfortable with."

Her sisters were ecstatic at that news.

"That is great," Kayla responded.

Kristen nodded in agreement. "I can't think of anybody better for you to fall for."

Keirra sighed. "Could I get just a little sympathy?"

Kayla shook her head while Kristen attempted to, but the effort was pitiful. Keirra frowned. "Is that all I get? After what I did when Randy almost broke your heart permanently?"

Kristen smiled. "I really appreciate what you did. If you and Eric ever have a fight, I will be by your side supporting you like you supported me."

Kayla shook her head again. "Well get ready. I am sure Keirra will find something to argue about even if she has to intentionally pick a fight with Eric."

Keirra wanted to kick her sister under the table, but she didn't want to give Kayla the satisfaction. Besides, Eric had yet to give her something to fight with him about, and it worried her. No one was that perfect.

Chapter Fourteen

Keirra came awake slowly as Eric's arms tightened around her. She could get used to being in his arms. Eric placed a kiss on her lips, and she smiled.

"Good morning," she whispered, still half asleep.

"Did you sleep well?"

She nodded and snuggled closer to him. "Yes, I did. You?"

"With you in my arms how could I not?"

He'd taken her out to eat last night before coming back to his place to watch movies until they had almost fallen asleep in front of the television. She had gone to bed with him simply holding her, and it had been a good night. One of the best that she'd had in a while. She rolled over onto her back and looked at Eric. His hair was tousled, and he had morning stubble. Sexiness oozed from him.

"You know I could wake up to you like this every day."

She looked at him, surprised at the statement. "What makes you say that?"

He laughed. "Because it's true." He smiled before lying back. "Tell me, Keirra, do you ever think of the future?"

She paused, having to think heavily about the question. To be honest, she always thought about the future, but the way she thought about it was starting to change. "Yes, I think about the future. I think about the future a lot."

"Do you think about kids and marriage?"

Keirra sat up. Her heart skipped a beat. That had been the last question she had expected, and it made her nervous, especially after the discussion she had just had with Kristen and Kayla over Randy taking Kristen to look at engagement rings.

She frowned. "What is making you ask this question?"

He reached out and stroked her arm. "Because regardless of what you think, I really am with you because I think we have a future together."

He pulled her back down beside him. "If I didn't, I wouldn't be here with you. Not like this."

Keirra was silent for a moment as she pondered his statement. It was a very believable one because he had brought her around his family when he barely knew her, and she fit in with them very well. She also knew he had never brought another woman home to meet his family. The whole situation was unnerving. Never had she thought that she would be having a conversation like this with Eric. He didn't seem like the sort to think about things like this, but she was realized her initial opinion of him had been way off.

She sighed softly but answered honestly. "Yes, I think about marriage as well as having children."

His hand began moving up and down in a soothing fashion. "How many children do you want to have?"

She didn't have to think about that answer. "At least two."

His hand stopped. "What is the maximum number?" He laughed at the expression that crossed her face. "I am just asking."

Keirra shrugged her shoulders. "To be honest, I don't have one. As long as my husband and I can afford the children and we are happy, then I think everything is okay."

He chuckled. "So you don't think that ten would be too many?"

That earned him a sharp elbow to the ribs. He grunted before laughing. "What? You said you didn't have a maximum."

She just shook her head. He could be so outrageous at times. She knew that he inherited his wacky sense of humor from his mother. She smiled as she relaxed back into his embrace.

"That may be, but that doesn't mean that I want to be pregnant for the rest of my life."

Even as she made the statement, she laughed. The man had a strange sense of humor, and quite frankly it was sexy. Everything about him was sexy.

She turned her head to look at him. "Why me, Eric? Out of all the women that you could have, why do you choose me?"

He responded without hesitation. "Because you are independent, unpredictable, caring, and sexy as hell."

Keirra smiled. She read the sincerity in his eyes. A sincerity that was hard to come by at times. Closing her eyes she tried to imagine waking up to Eric every morning. What shocked her was the image came to her mind very clearly. It was then that she realized that she had done exactly what she said that she wasn't going to do. She had fallen in love with Eric.

* * * *

Keirra half ran, half walked into the entrance of school. Technically, she was still early but not as early as she wanted to be. She was barely going to have enough time to prepare for class before it started. After walking into the office, she signed in before heading into her classroom. The first bell rang as she began to put the scales on the tables that her students shared. When the tardy bell rang, everything was set up.

The first class went well, and she had a few minutes to breathe before the second class started. A smile came to her face when her planning period rolled around. She needed it. By the end of the school day she exhaled heavily. Her cell phone rang as soon as she exited the building. A smile spread over her face when Eric's name appeared on the caller ID.

Her heart rate sped up with excitement. His voice was always a highlight of her day. She flipped the phone open. "Hey, you."

"Hey yourself."

Her smile widened at his sexy timbre. "What are you doing?"

"Watching a beautiful woman walk to her car."

At that statement, she stopped and looked around. It didn't take her long to spot him. He was standing by his patrol car with his hat pulled low. His profile made her heart speed up. The man was already sexy as sin, but in uniform, he was something else. His body was definitely made for the uniform. She headed in his direction hanging up the phone as she neared him. He pulled her into his embrace as soon as she was within arm's reach. His lips were on hers before she could take her next breath.

It was a brief kiss, but it didn't lack passion. He pulled back taking her bag out of her hands. Being such a perfect gentleman made him even harder to resist.

"Did you have a good day?"

She nodded as he placed her bag into the car then assisted her inside, before going around to the driver's side and got in. He drove her the short distance to her car.

"How was your day?"

He gave her a dry look, and she laughed. "You missing the fast-paced criminals of the city?"

He shook his head. "Believe it or not, I don't, but I swear if Mrs. Shiloh places one more non-emergency call, I will lock her up myself."

She laughed until she had tears in her eyes. "I think there is a law against locking up seventy-year-old women for no reason."

He scoffed at her comment. "Well, I *know* there is one against sexual harassment. There is nothing innocent about the woman. She is a sexual predator."

Keirra gave him a look of surprise. "What are you talking about?"

He sighed. "Mrs. Shiloh always makes a special request for me and manages to pinch my butt every time I walk by."

She began to laugh again at his look of contempt.

"I am glad you find this so funny."

She shook her head. Just thinking about Mrs. Shiloh grabbing Eric's butt was a sight she had to see. She was well aware of how much of a feisty woman Mrs. Shiloh was, she believed the woman would be bold enough to feel a uniform officer up.

"Would it make you feel better if I had a talk with Mrs. Shiloh?"

"Ha! That woman will probably beat you up then come find me for ratting her out."

Keirra had to put her head in her lap to keep from hyperventilating. When she was able to control herself again, she leaned over and gave him another kiss to console him. "I am sorry. I know this isn't funny."

He gave her a slightly irritated look. "Then why are you laughing?"

She didn't respond. She wouldn't be able to complete the statement without laughing. Instead, she just stared at him until he had to smile himself.

"I forgive you this time." He leaned over and gave her another kiss. "As much as I hate to go, I need to get back to work."

"What time are you getting off?"

He grinned. "Seven, and yes, I will call you."

She smiled. "I will talk to you then, and thank you for coming to see me."

He got out of the patrol car and went around to the passenger side. He opened the door, and she stepped out. He reached in and he grabbed her bag before handing it to her. Leaning forward, she placed a kiss on his lips before heading for her own car. She didn't know what she'd done to get so lucky, but she was grateful.

* * * *

With one last kiss, Eric went back around to the driver's side and climbed back into the car. He watched her drive off before heading back to the station. As soon as he walked in, a smile came to his face. Randy was in his office with his feet up on his desk. His cell phone was to his ear, and judging by the grin on his face, he was on the phone with Kristen. Randy saw him and cut his conversation with Kristen short but not before speaking to Wade. Eric found himself becoming jealous. Randy had a lot going for himself. He wanted that with Keirra.

"So how was patrol?"

Eric gave Randy a look before sitting down in an empty chair. "If I have to respond to one more of Mrs. Shiloh's non-emergency calls, I'm going to quit."

Randy chuckled. "She likes your butt too, huh?"

Eric could only shake his head in response. "The only good thing that came out of the patrol today was that I ran into Keirra."

Randy smiled and leaned back in his chair. "How is that going?"

He nodded. "I think things are going very well."

Randy gave him an incredulous look. "Only good? I guess you can say that, but I don't know if you realize just how much Keirra has changed."

Eric looked at Randy. "Randy you have no idea how much she has changed me."

Chapter Fifteen

"Why are you so nervous?"

She looked at Eric and sighed. "I have no idea."

Truth was her heart was in her stomach because her paternal grandparents were going to be in town momentarily. They were coming for the sole purpose of meeting Eric. Evidently, Kristen had mentioned that she and Eric were dating, and her grandparents wanted to meet the man who had managed to get behind the wall she had put up. She jumped a foot in the air when the doorbell rang. Eric laughed before squeezing her hand.

"Relax. Everything is going to be fine."

She took a deep breath before opening the door. A smile automatically came to her face when she saw her grandparents.

"Grandma, Grandpa!"

She stepped forward to embrace her grandparents. She had been looking forward to their arrival all morning. Each of them hugged her tightly before stepping inside the house.

"We are so glad you could make it."

Her grandmother gave her grandfather a look. "Well thanks to your grandfather, we almost didn't."

Keirra found herself rolling her eyes and wondering what story they were going to hear over dinner tonight.

Her grandfather gave her grandmother his own look but ignored the statement as he embraced Keirra.

"Where are your sisters?"

She squeezed her grandfather tightly. "They are going to meet us at Jimmy's."

Her grandfather rubbed his hands together in anticipation. "Well if that is the case, what are we waiting for?"

Keirra shook her head. "How about an introduction to Eric? You know, the guy that you came here to meet," she stated with a smile.

It wasn't until then that her grandparents realized Eric was in the room with them. He had stood beside her quiet until that point. Stepping forward, he greeted her grandparents.

"Mr. and Mrs. Smith, it is a pleasure to meet you."

Her grandmother waved her hand in dismissal. "Oh none of that Mr. and Mrs. stuff. Call us Grandma and Grandpa. You are part of the family now."

Keirra groaned as Eric smiled and went along with the suggestion.

"Well then it is a pleasure to meet you, Grandma and Grandpa."

As she expected, her grandmother almost melted at the first hint of his charm. "Hopefully, you have heard good things about us."

He laughed as he embraced her grandmother and shook her grandfather's hand. "I have heard nothing but good things about you."

Sensing that her grandmother was getting ready to request examples she stepped forward and interrupted. It could be dangerous if her grandmother became talkative.

"And on that note we have people waiting on us so we need to get going."

Eric took the hint and led the way to his SUV assisting her and her grandparents into his vehicle before climbing into the driver's seat.

They made it to Jimmy's without incident, and she sighed with relief. Her sisters, Randy, and Wade were waiting impatiently when they walked into Jimmy's. Poor Wade was staring with longing at other tables that had pizza on them. The smell of the pizza distracted her while her sisters greeted their grandparents.

She waited as her grandparents talked to Kayla and Keirra smiling to herself. As she had figured her grandparents would, they found Eric to be perfect. He became the person of the hour charming them like he charmed her. A short while later they placed the orders for their pizza. They decided to eat at Jimmy's because everyone wanted pizza, and Jimmy's had the best that there was. As soon as they were seated orders were taken, and the pictures came out. Her grandparents began sharing the photos of their recent travels, and funny stories were spread around the table.

Keirra sat back and watched her family. She loved times like these because she didn't feel so lonely. There were times that she was starved for her own family. Not that her sisters didn't count, but the pain of not having a mother and father made her cherish her surviving grandparents even more, especially since they were the parents of her father. Seeing them always brought back good memories of the special bond that she'd had with her father, of the bond she had with them. But she was starting to really think about a family of her own.

"What are you thinking about?"

She looked over at Eric when he spoke to her. He always seemed to know when something was on her mind. He insisted that her eyes and body posture gave her away. She knew it was probably true. As a little girl when she looked into her father's eyes, she had always known what he had been thinking. Even the night that he had been shot, she had been able to read the fear and the pain in his eyes. It had been something she had never forgotten.

At the time, she hadn't known what the expression had meant, but eventually, she realized her father had known he wasn't going to be with them much longer. In a way, she had known it as well. She looked up as Eric reached over and squeezed her hand.

"Whatever it is, try not to think about it. Your grandparents are here, and you are supposed to be enjoying yourself."

She smiled at him and nodded. "You are right. I am starting to get wrinkles from frowning so much."

She turned her attention back to her grandparents and laughed at her grandmother's reenactment of her grandfather's run-in with a deer. For some reason, her grandparents always seemed to have collisions with wildlife. It also seemed that her grandfather could move quicker than it looked. This was also the story that her grandmother had been making reference to earlier.

Their pizzas arrived, and they ate. Then it was their turn to share their stories of anything interesting that had occurred lately. The highlight of the subject was Kayla and her attraction to James. Keirra teased Kayla to the point that she threatened to poison her ice cream. Everyone let up, but the conversation became serious the next time her grandmother spoke.

"Does this man know you are attracted to him?"

Kayla sighed. "Grandma, he would have to be blind not to."

Kayla retold the story of her encounter with James Feldon, and their grandparents leaned back in their chairs to listen. When she was finished they stared at her. "Sounds like a match made in heaven."

Keirra looked over at Eric when her grandmother made the statement. He held Wade, and from the looks of it they were in a deep conversation with each other. Eric was listening intently to every word that Wade said. Her heart melted at the sight, and it was easy to imagine him taking the time and effort with his own children. He was definitely good with children in a way she would have never expected him to be. She would have thought he would have run off in the opposite direction at the thought of having to spend time with a child.

Her grandmother's words to Kayla echoed in her head. What she had with him seemed to be a match made in heaven. She knew there was a risk when she had gotten involved with Eric. For some reason, dating an officer of the law bothered her but not as much. What scared her more now, was their relationship was working out well, too well. Right now, his job wasn't the main issue because nothing had happened for it to be. Would his job ever become a strain on their relationship? If it did, could their relationship survive?

* * * *

"I have got to be losing my mind."

Keirra said it more to herself than to anyone else. She was getting her suitcase ready for the trip to Atlanta. In the middle of the process, she began to doubt her sanity. Yet, she had good reason. Knowing that she was going to be spending four days with his family was a little nerve-racking. One full day was fine, but four might be too much. After doing a quick check she zipped up the bag and sat it by the door. Eric would be there any moment. She grabbed her purse and suitcase before heading downstairs as quietly as possible. It was early, and she didn't want to wake Kayla. She would call her a little later. Just as she made it downstairs she saw Eric's headlights pull up into the yard. She put her coat on and headed out the front door. Eric ran up to pick up her suitcase. Together they walked to his SUV. He opened the door then gave her a brief kiss on the lips. She slid into the vehicle with his help.

Eric placed her suitcase in the trunk then went around and slid in on the driver's side. "Good morning."

She smiled. "Good morning."

"You can take your coat off before I start driving if you want. I will have the heater on."

She took off the coat and secured her seatbelt. When she was finished, he backed out of the driveway, and they were on their way to Atlanta.

"You might want to sleep on the way down. We are going to eat early."

She nodded again and closed her eyes, but sleep didn't come, and it should have. When they made it to Atlanta, her eyes were still wide open. Eric pulled up to his parents' home. He got their bags and made his way up the walkway. Arthur opened the door with a warm smile.

"*Buenos días.* Come on in, you two."

They stepped into the house, and Keirra inhaled as she embraced Arthur. "Something smells really good."

She hadn't eaten breakfast, and it may have been a mistake because her stomach was about to embarrass her. Arthur must have read her mind.

"You two put your things up, and come and join Charlotte and myself in the kitchen."

Eric nodded and led her down the hall. She looked at him in surprise when he led her past the guest room she had stayed in last time. Instead, he led her to his room. She shook her head.

"*Oh no.* Absolutely not."

Eric laughed. "Sometimes I think that is your favorite phrase."

She gave him a look of warning. "Well, most of the time, I think you are insane, and where has it gotten us?"

Her comment made him laugh even harder, but he continued into his room. She tried to take her bag from him but quickly discovered she was wasting her time.

She rolled her eyes in irritation. "I refuse to sleep with you in your parents' home."

"What is wrong with us sleeping in the same room?"

She crossed her arms over her chest. "Nothing if it was actually sleeping you were thinking about doing."

He stared at her with mock disappointment. "You wound me."

Ready to do battle, she glared at him, but her stomach grumbled. "We will take this matter up once my stomach is full."

He smiled and sat the bags down. She allowed him to lead the way to the kitchen. Charlotte had their plates ready, and Keirra sat down with a grateful thank-you in Spanish to Charlotte. A smile appeared on Charlotte's face.

"You have been working on your Spanish."

She gave a slightly embarrassed nod. "Eric has taught me a few phrases and words, but I can't hold a conversation beyond a greeting yet."

Eric grinned. "She is a good student, and she will be able to hold a conversation in no time."

She felt a sense of warmth at his compliment as she began to eat, savoring the ham, eggs, and English muffins. She could tell he had been surprised when she'd asked him to teach her a few words of Spanish. As she stated earlier, it would take her some time to be able to hold a conversation, but she could probably walk around the kitchen and pronounce a few items in the kitchen, including those on her plate. Several minutes later, she pushed the plate away. Eric's hand snaked out and grabbed the piece of ham and English muffin she had left on her plate, and they disappeared into his mouth before she could blink.

"You need any help, Mother?"

Charlotte nodded her head in the direction of the uncooked turkey. "You can stuff your brother."

Eric laughed before standing up. He grabbed his plate and hers to take them to the sink. He washed his hands, and then dried them before patting the turkey.

"I will take good care of you."

Keirra laughed. Delusion definitely ran in his family, which is why he fit so well into her own. A yawn escaped her, and she covered her mouth just in time to avoid being rude.

"Why don't you go lie down and rest?"

Keirra shook her head. She would feel guilty about sleeping while everyone else worked. "I couldn't leave you guys to do all the work."

Charlotte waved a hand of dismissal. "The only thing that I'm preparing is the turkey and the cornbread stuffing."

Eric nodded solemnly. "It is true, and I am taking care of the turkey, so it only leaves Mom with the dressing."

"My daughters are making the vegetables and dessert."

Feeling reassured that she wouldn't leave the impression of a bad guest, she stood. She thanked Charlotte for breakfast, before walking over to give Eric a kiss, amazed at how easy the action came to her. She headed to Eric's room, and she knew she should take her bag and head to the guest room but his bed looked so inviting. Maybe she should sit on it to see if it felt as comfortable as it looked. It did. As a matter of fact, it felt more comfortable than the guest room bed did. She couldn't resist lying down. The bed was really comfortable. So comfortable that she fell asleep without realizing it.

* * * *

"Oh my goodness, everything looks great," Keirra murmured.

Eric rubbed his hands in anticipation. "Yeah, but it tastes even better than it looks."

Keirra stared at the food that covered the table and automatically thought about her sisters. She had talked to them briefly before sitting down to dinner with the Brooks. The one comfort she had was knowing her sisters were enjoying their dinner with the Strouds.

Charlotte beamed. "Thank you, dear. Now who is going to bless the food?"

Eric volunteered to do it. He took Keirra's hand in his and blessed the food quickly and efficiently. Soon food was being passed around, and Eric made her plate putting everything she asked for on it. The first bite of food had her closing her eyes in pleasure. Everything tasted good.

"Are you okay?"

She looked up at Eric and grinned. "Yes, I am. I am glad you invited me."

"I am glad you came," Eric stated before he brushed a kiss across her lips.

"Ooh, Uncle Eric and Keirra are kissing at the table."

Keirra laughed at Nina. Eric made a goofy face, and it made Nina laugh along with a few other members of the family.

"Did you have a chance to talk to your sisters?"

Keirra smiled at Irene's question before nodding. "Yes, I did. They told me to tell all of you hello."

"Maybe we will get a chance to meet them soon," Gaia added.

Marianne grinned. "I am anxious to see if I can tell you guys apart."

Eric laughed. "Trust me, you can. They might look alike, but that is where the similarity ends."

Keirra shook her head. "Your brother is one of a kind. He was able to tell us apart from day one. There are people who have known us for years and can't tell us apart."

Owen laughed. "My brother and I are three years apart, and people think that we are twins."

Gaia rolled her eyes. "Those people are blind. You and your brother look nothing alike."

Keirra found herself laughing. They were comical.

"Well maybe we can meet your sisters when we come to Baxley for Christmas," Charlotte announced with a smile.

That caused Eric to look up quickly. There was a sincere look of alarm on his face, and Keirra tried not to laugh. It was nice to see the tables turned on him for once. His mother only smiled.

"What did you say?"

Charlotte looked at her son with innocence. "Well how long did you think it would be before we would come and visit you at your new home?"

Eric arched a dark brow in his mother's direction. "Normally you ask a person if you can invade their house before you do it."

Keirra tried to hide her amusement. "Yes, Eric. Just like you ask people where they want to go for the holidays."

He issued her a warning glare, and she promptly ignored it. It only served him right for all of the headaches that he'd caused her with his underhanded scheming.

Arthur laughed. "You know your mother. She doesn't ask to do anything, not when she doesn't have to."

Arthur managed to dodge Charlotte's hand, and Eric looked at Keirra for assistance. She shrugged her shoulders. There was no way she was going to go up against the Brooks. There were times when she didn't go up against her sisters, and she was only outnumbered by two to one there.

"Traitor," he muttered, and she laughed.

"That may be, but I am on the winning side, and now I know where you get it from."

Laughter sounded from around the table, and she watched Eric shake his head. Unfortunately, he was fighting a losing battle, and she could tell that he knew it. He gave her another look of irritation, and she smiled.

"It looks like you will have a full house for Christmas."

Chapter Sixteen

Keirra looked up as Eric's cell phone rang. She hadn't realized how deep in thought she'd been. He looked at the caller ID and grinned before answering the phone. Even though she was sitting next to him, she only caught bits and pieces of the conversation as Eric talked. He put the caller on hold before looking over at her.

"Keirra, would you like to go out to eat with a couple of my friends?"

She gave him a look surprise. They had spent the day relaxing, and she was still trying to recover from yesterday's Thanksgiving dinner. She had enjoyed spending time with his parents and listening to the amusing stories they had about Eric as a child. He had turned a dark shade of red under his tan when his mother brought out the photo book, but he had been a good sport.

After the photo book had been put away, Arthur had dragged Charlotte off upstairs and left them to watch movies in the family room. She and Eric didn't have any plans, which was why an invite to dinner tonight had been the last thing she'd expected. "When?"

"Tonight."

Her eyes widened, but she found herself nodding. What was she going to wear? Eric confirmed they would be joining his friends before ending the call. He hung up the phone.

"What is wrong?"

She sighed. "Unfortunately, I didn't bring anything nice to wear out, so I need to run to the mall."

Eric smiled in return. "Well I despise shopping and only do it when I absolutely have to, but I know just the people that can help."

Eric reopened the phone and dialed his oldest sister's number. Gaia answered on the first ring.

"Hey, Gaia, how is it going?"

He paused for Gaia's response before continuing. "Good. I have a huge favor to ask. Keirra and I will be joining a few friends for dinner tonight. However, Keirra doesn't have anything to wear."

Eric chuckled and looked at the phone before putting it back in his pocket. She looked at him with puzzlement.

"What happened?"

"Nothing. Gaia and the rest of my sisters will be here shortly to take you to find something. I say you have about thirty minutes to get ready before my sisters show up."

Keirra nodded. She was already dressed. All she had to do was put on her shoes. Exactly thirty minutes later, she found out Eric had been right on with his guess when the doorbell rang. Eric opened the door, and his sisters entered the house noisily. They greeted him before turning their attention to her. Each of them hugged her, and she couldn't help but smile.

"How long do we have to get her ready?"

Eric looked at his watch. "From the time we need to leave till now you guys have four hours total."

Gaia grinned. "We will see you back here in two."

Keirra's lips had barely touched Eric's before Gaia, Irene, and Marianne were rushing her out of the house. They loaded her in Gaia's SUV.

"Where are we going?"

Gaia laughed. "The question should be where aren't we going. There are a few places we have in mind. We are going to start at the mall, but I don't think we are going to find what we need there. There is also a boutique I have in mind."

Keirra could only nod as Gaia backed out of the driveway. "Well, I have to be honest. I'm not a shopper. That duty falls on Kristen's shoulders."

Irene laughed. "That is okay. We are, and by the time we get through with you today, you will be one as well."

Keirra smiled. If Kristen could see her now she would probably laugh. Gaia made it to the mall and found a good parking spot. They made their way into the mall.

"Is there any particular color you like?"

Keirra shrugged her shoulders. "When my sister picks something out for me, she always chooses the color green or purple."

Marianne tilted her head to the side as if trying to imagine her in the colors. "I can see those colors on you. Normally a darker shade of green or purple right?"

Keirra laughed. "My sister Kristen would love to come shopping with you.

I think the two of you, actually all of you, would have fun."

Eric's sisters laughed at her as they entered the mall, and Gaia led everyone in the direction of a dress shop. Keirra walked around the store listening to the sisters' tips before picking out a few dresses she wanted to try on. She made her way to the dressing room. After trying on the four dresses, she frowned.

They were all nice, but not what she was in search of. Gaia, Irene, and Marianne agreed with her. She redressed, and they left the store.

Gaia checked her watch. "There is one more store I think we should check out before we go to the boutique."

When everyone agreed, Marianne led everyone to another store. They had barely been in the store when Keirra spotted the dress that was for her. She went to the rack and picked up the spearmint-colored, knee-length, chiffon halter-back dress.

"I love this."

"Good choice," Gaia stated.

Keirra searched for her size on the rack before picking up the dress. She went into the dressing room. As soon as she did, she knew that the dress was hers. When she stepped out of the dressing room, Gaia, Irene, and Marianne confirmed what she already knew.

"That looks great on you," Marianne replied.

Keirra smiled. "I am getting this one."

She went back into the dressing room and took the dress off. A look at the price tag made her feel faint. She redressed and exited the dressing room. Gaia took the dress out of her hands.

"Now we need accessories."

Keirra reached out and caught Gaia before she could run off. "The dress is a little out of my price range."

Marianne laughed. "Don't worry about the price of the dress."

Irene put her arm around Keirra's shoulder. "My little brother is funding today's shopping spree. So tell us, is there anything else you need to go with this lovely dress?"

She hesitated at the thought of Eric spending so much money on a dress. It was a sweet gesture that was appreciated. Marianne read the apprehension in her expression, and she gave her a gentle smile.

"My brother just wants to make sure you have a good time tonight, so let him spoil you by doing this one little thing."

Marianne's simple words affected her in a positive way. She had never really splurged on herself, and she definitely hadn't dated anyone who had wanted to splurge on her. Everything about Eric was genuine, and if he volunteered the money to purchase an outfit for her to enjoy herself, she wasn't going to argue the point. She looked at the three expectant faces before her and smiled. "Okay, I will take the dress, and I need a strapless bra, but I will pay for it."

His sisters exchanged a look between them before nodding, and Gaia grabbed her hand. "That is fine. We will grab one of those as well."

They purchased the dress before heading to a lingerie shop. She picked up the strapless bra that she needed, and they bought it as well, which caused another argument that she lost because she was outnumbered, and they threatened to call Eric and tell him that she was being uncooperative. The threat alone was enough to make her give in. She also saw where Eric learned his negotiation skills from for his sisters were definitely professionals.

"Now we just need accessories," Irene added.

"I have a purse," Keirra interjected with a look of horror at the thought of having to search for another. The one she had was good enough. She hardly carried it, so it was in good shape.

All three sisters burst out laughing. Gaia shook her head. "You have a lot to learn about accessories."

By the time they left the mall, she had. She had everything she needed for the night. When they climbed into Gaia's SUV, she almost freaked out at the amount of time that had elapsed. It didn't seem as if they had spent over two hours in the mall shopping, but they had. When they pulled into the driveway, Eric opened the door. He was looking at his watch as they walked up the driveway.

"You guys cut it pretty close, didn't you?"

Marianne gave him a kiss on the cheek. "If you had truly been worried, then you would have called. Besides, when you see Keirra, it will be worth it."

Gaia slapped Eric's hand when he reached out to touch the shopping bags. "No peeking. You will see what we bought soon enough."

Irene took Keirra's arm. "Now we are going to go upstairs and start getting ready."

Eric gave them his most pitiful look, and even Keirra found herself rolling her eyes.

"Can I at least know the color to see if I have a tie that matches?"

"Green," all three of his sisters replied in unison before pulling Keirra up the stairs.

"We will use my old room," Irene volunteered.

They entered the room and closed the door. When all three women turned to face her, she smiled.

"Thank you guys for all of your help."

"Who said that we were finished?" Marianne asked.

Keirra laughed as she shrugged. "Well, you guys have already done so much, and I just assumed that you were finished."

Gaia shook her head. "We are going to stay and help you get dressed."

Keirra smiled. "Well I need to get my toiletry bag from the room."

Irene volunteered to get it. Marianne turned back to look at her. "Well that is taken care of. Now you aren't shy, are you?"

Keirra shook her head. She had dressed and undressed in front of her sisters, and as much time as she had spent with the trio lately she considered Gaia, Irene, and Marianne like her sisters. Gaia handed her the bag that had her underwear in it.

"We will be waiting for you out here."

She nodded and walked into the bathroom. Once she stepped from the tub she dried off and slid into the underwear. Marianne had talked her into buying a pair of underwear that matched the strapless bra. A glance in the mirror told her that Eric would probably give up enchiladas at Sam's Café at the chance to see her right now. She wrapped the towel around herself and opened the door to the bathroom. Gaia, Irene, and Marianne were standing there expectantly. They handed her the dress, and she slipped into it quickly. As soon as the dress fell into place she knew she had made the right choice. The dress had been made for her. It hugged every curve it was supposed to.

Irene laughed. "Eric isn't going to let you out of the house."

Keirra laughed. "He isn't going to have a choice. I am starving."

The women shared a laugh before Irene handed her the new shoes. She slipped into the shoes and immediately fell in love with them. Marianne rubbed her hands together in anticipation.

"It is time for hair and makeup."

By the time they finished, Keirra had tears in her eyes, and they had a minute to spare. She was embarrassed at the unexpected emotion and tried to hide it unsuccessfully.

"Don't cry on us. We won't have time to fix your makeup," Gaia scolded her playfully.

Keirra laughed. She felt beautiful, very beautiful. Gaia showed her how to blot her eyes without ruining the makeup. When Marianne returned, she had in her hands the simple necklace she had picked out. As simple as it looked in her hand, once it was around her neck, plain wouldn't describe the necklace.

"You look so beautiful," Irene said around a smile.

Marianne grinned. "Yes, you do. Now we need to get you downstairs so you can leave our brother speechless."

Keirra nodded, knowing what Marianne said was true. Each of the women gave her a kiss on the cheek. "You come downstairs after us."

Keirra watched the three women leave the room. She took a deep breath before standing. Never would she have thought she would be this nervous about impressing Eric. Standing up, she smoothed her dress before heading out of the room. She reached the top of the stairs and stopped. Eric was speaking with his sisters, but as if sensing she was near, he looked up, and his eyes landed on her. The expression on his face was priceless. He broke away from his sisters and moved toward the bottom of the stairs.

"You look beautiful," he whispered.

"Thank you."

Eric took her hand in his before turning to face his sisters. "Thank you all for your help today. We have to get going. I will talk to you guys tomorrow."

He led her toward the door, and she turned to thank Gaia, Irene, and Marianne once more.

"You are more than welcome. Just promise us you two will have a great time."

They left with the promise that they would. Eric assisted her into his SUV. She couldn't help but to notice how sexy he looked himself. He had on a dark, charcoal-colored suit with a white shirt and a green tie that almost matched her dress perfectly. He couldn't have planned the outfit better. The drive to the restaurant was a short one.

"Have you ever been to Tomás' before?"

Keirra smiled at his question. "We left Atlanta when we were ten."

Eric grinned. "Well then, you are in for a treat."

He pulled up in front of the restaurant and let valet take his SUV. Taking her hand in his he led her into the restaurant. They were led to the table where six other people were already seated. There were handshakes, hugs, and cheek kisses going all around the tables as she was introduced to Santos, Christy, Oscar, Ramona, Harris, and Mirabel, all of them friend's he'd had since college.

The meal was entertaining, and she felt welcome within the group. Sitting and listening to their stories had her laughing. One of the things she picked up on was that the Eric she knew was the Eric he had always been. She liked that. At the end of dinner, Eric made her get a decadent chocolate dessert she didn't need, but he split it with her, which eased her guilty conscious somewhat.

"We need to go dancing," Mirabel said.

Both Keirra and Eric paused in the middle of the bite that they were taking. She shrugged because she really didn't care. Right now, she was having a good time with Eric, and she wasn't ready for it to end.

Chapter Seventeen

Keirra looked around the club that Eric and his friends had brought her to. She wasn't even certain that it could be called a club. It looked to be more of a bar with an intimate dance floor, intimate being the key word. The few people that were on the dance floor were a moment away from being arrested. Their dancing could only be described as provocative. She could see why though. The beat of the music was addictive, and she found herself swaying to it on occasion. She took another sip of the fruity concoction that Eric had ordered for her. The name of the drink had slipped her mind, but it was good. She was taking her time in drinking the alcoholic beverage because she wasn't a heavy drinker by any means. A glass of wine or one beer was normally what she had, and she could count on one hand how many she'd had for the year. Her attention went to Oscar and Ramona as they stood and headed for the dance floor. The couple moved together in unison so closely that she turned her attention to Eric to give them the privacy she felt they needed.

He had undressed slightly since they left Tomás's. His suit jacket was in the SUV along with his tie. He had unbuttoned the top two buttons on his shirt, which revealed silky chest hair that she liked to play with when she and Eric lay in bed at night. She liked the look on him. He was a sexy man, and there was no denying it. A few moments later, a popular song by Shakira that she liked came on. She couldn't help but to sway to the song. When she looked up she found him smiling at her.

"Do you want to dance?"

It was hard to hide her surprise. Not because she had never danced with him, but because she had never danced with anyone to Latin music. She had danced by herself in private, but that wasn't an option here. She shook her head. "I'm not really sure about this. I have never actually danced to this music with anyone before."

Eric smiled. "That doesn't matter. We danced well together the last time, so this should be easy. Trust me."

Eric stood and held out his hand. Keirra hesitated wanting to point out that country music was different from Latin music, but she trusted him, so she reached out, took his hand, and allowed him to assist her to her feet. He led her to the dance floor.

"Just feel the music."

His hands dropped to her hips, and Keirra followed his lead effortlessly. Soon they were moving together with ease. They were so close there was hardly any room for their clothes to fit. The man could definitely move his hips. Keirra did a slow and sensuous turn that placed her back against his front. She looked at him over her shoulder, and his gaze met hers. The lustful look in his eyes matched the one that was in hers. She moved to the beat of the music and enjoyed the way she felt. She was getting turned on . . . a lot.

The music must have affected him as well because Eric's hands began roaming over her body in a way that should be reserved for the bedroom. Right now, she didn't care. Eric's hands found her hips again and turned her until she was facing him. A second later, his lips found hers. He distracted her to the point where she didn't hear the beat of the music change. When it did, Eric automatically picked up the new beat, and she followed him. Keirra finally had to pull back when she needed a good breath of air. Their lips didn't stay separated long. The next time either one of them spoke was when the song ended.

"Are you ready to go home?" His voice was raspy with desire.

Keirra nodded slowly, knowing exactly what he meant. He gave her another brief kiss before taking her hand and leading her off the floor. They stopped by the table and said a brief good-bye with the promise of getting together again soon.

Eric led her outside, stopping to place another passionate kiss on her lips. When she felt almost boneless, he let her go before leading her to the SUV. He helped her in and then went around to get in on the other side. The drive home was a quick one, and Eric was pulling into his parents' driveway several minutes later. Keirra had to admit she had been concerned about what Eric would think about how she looked earlier. The combination of his expression when he saw her at the top of the stairs and their interaction a few minutes ago took away all doubt that was there. He always told her how beautiful she was, but when he looked at her that was when she knew. Eric turned off the engine and got out. By the time he made it around to the passenger side, she already had the door open. She was in Eric's arms before the door was even closed.

He scooped her up into his arms, and his lips barely left her as he headed toward the front door. Minutes later, he had both of them upstairs in his bedroom. He set her on her feet before locking the door.

"You are beautiful."

She smiled and wrapped her arms around his neck. "Thank you. You look very handsome yourself."

Eric grinned wickedly as he stepped closer to her. "Thank you. Now I think we should pick up where we left off."

"I agree," Keirra murmured as she tilted her head back to give Eric the perfect angle to press his lips against hers. He picked her up and carried her toward the bed. When he stood her on her feet, she automatically reached for his shirt. Her hands paused for a moment.

"How did you manage to find a tie that almost matched my dress?"

He chuckled and shrugged his shoulders. "I didn't have one to be honest, but Dad did, so I borrowed his."

Keirra studied him for a moment before smiling. "Well, I think green is your color."

Eric laughed. "I am glad you think so because it is definitely yours."

Keirra looked down at the chest hair that had teased her all night before undoing the buttons to his shirt. She tugged his shirt out of his pants and continued until she had no more buttons to undo. The sight of his chest did something to her. His stomach contracted, and muscles rippled at her touch. That was all that it took. Seconds later, he had both of them stripped naked and in the bed. She made him slow down when she caught sight of his arousal. Her hands slid toward his thick and pulsing erection, and he couldn't do anything but moan. She smiled at the proof of his wanting her. He wanted her just as much as she wanted him.

When she touched the tip of his erection, his self-control disappeared. Before she could blink, Eric had her pinned underneath him. Her thighs automatically separated, and she arched against him trying to give herself the sensation that she craved. He moved slightly denying her the goal that she was trying to achieve. She watched him reach for his wallet and pull out protection. He began to roll the protection on, and she couldn't help but to watch every move. She reached for him, but he stopped her.

When she went to protest, he came over her and pushed deep inside of her. Keirra gasped, arching into him. Every time he entered her, it seemed to get better and better. He withdrew and thrust again causing her to moan. She tightened her grip on him, and he spoke into her ear. He spoke words of Spanish. They were words that turned her on to the point of insanity. The more Eric talked, the more she became turned on. She had made the mistake and confided how much it aroused her to hear him speak it, and he had used it against her ever since. Keirra's head fell back, and her grip on him tightened even more.

Her legs circled him, and she tilted her hips into his, taking him deeper. A second later she gasped as she went over the edge. Eric's mouth covered hers, muffling her cries of pleasure that followed as well as his own moans of pleasure.

When he could summon enough energy to move he rolled to the side pulling her with him. She loved the feel of his body against hers, although she wouldn't admit it aloud. One thing she figured out was she could show Eric how she felt even if she couldn't tell him. She wasn't good with words. Unfortunately she never had been. When it came to trying to express herself on a personal level, she was incapable of getting herself together enough to do it.

"Did you have a good time tonight?"

Keirra couldn't help but laugh, and a moment later, Eric's laughter joined hers. "You ought to try to get your mind out of the gutter sometimes."

Keirra found herself rolling her eyes. "Trust me. My mind isn't in the gutter until I am around you."

Eric went up on one elbow. "Then it is a good thing."

He smiled, and she felt her heart flutter. It never failed to amaze her at how sexy Eric was. It could easily become a habit to stare at him all day, and that bothered her. She was falling harder and harder for Eric every day. What made it even worse was how well she fit in with his family. That worried her a little. She didn't want to find more reasons that would keep her with Eric. He couldn't be this perfect. There had to be a few reasons as to why she shouldn't be with him. Unfortunately, she hadn't found any.

* * * *

Eric watched as Keirra gasped, and her eyes flew open as her body convulsed in pleasure. His hands had a firm grip on her hips only confirming that even though she had been asleep she hadn't been dreaming. Her body continued to clench and the low sounds of pleasure that he seem to love to hear from her fell from her throat. His tongue continued to delve into the very essence of her, loving her.

"Eric!"

Her muffled scream reached his ears as the pleasure intensified. When he looked up, he smiled. She was sure she did look comical since she had placed the pillow over her mouth to mute her sounds of pleasure. He came up over her, removed the pillow, and replaced it with his mouth. He staked his claim hungrily, and Keirra felt her breathing quicken. Eric's kiss told her he wanted her with everything he had. He was in control, and she followed his lead. Her arms came up, and she wrapped them around Eric.

He ended the kiss before lowering his mouth to her breast. She matched his passion with her own.

"I want you inside of me. Now!"

Eric reached for protection and put it on quickly. When he entered her, she moaned in pleasure. Eric smiled at the sound before moving deeper within her. Keirra inhaled sharply before inching back a little.

"Too much," she gasped.

Eric eased up a little and started up a rhythm that still had her gasping. It wasn't long before she went over the edge taking him with her. The sensation of experiencing the ultimate release with him was one that she would never tire of. He rolled to the side pulling her with him. This trip had been a good one. Yet, it was getting harder to deny that they belonged together.

She knew he felt the same way, but she was still fighting to keep her heart closed to him. Unfortunately, he didn't seem to plan on letting her have her way.

"What do we have planned for today?" Keirra asked still breathless from their lovemaking.

"I want to swing by the police station and say hello to a few people."

Keirra stiffened as soon as the words were out of his mouth. "The police station?"

He smiled. "The one and only."

Keirra was silent a moment. She wondered if she looked as horrified as she felt. She had been uncertain of when this day would come, but it had, and she would face it head on. Taking a deep calming breath, she looked over at him.

"When are we leaving?"

He stretched. "After we take a shower and eat breakfast."

Keirra nodded and slid out of bed before heading for the bathroom. She turned on the water and stepped under the spray once it was the right temperature. Leaning heavily against the wall, she took care not to get her hair wet. She couldn't believe what she had just agreed to. To be truthful, it wasn't like she had a lot of choice. She had to face her past at some time, especially if she ever wanted to have a normal future. Taking a deep breath she began bathing. The quicker she got ready, the quicker she could get this over with.

By the time she finished, her nerves were better. She turned off the water before climbing out of the shower. Eric had put on a pair of boxer briefs and was walking around the bedroom. The sad thing was that her body automatically reacted to the sight of his. Instead of going after him like she wanted to, she went to the closet and pulled out a sweater bearing the logo of her alma mater and a pair of jeans.

"Will we be doing a lot of walking?"

Eric shook his head before disappearing into the bathroom. She slipped her feet into ankle-high boots and headed back into the bathroom. She brushed her teeth, and by the time she was finished Eric had stepped out of the shower. When they made it into the kitchen, Keirra's nerves were racing again. Arthur and Charlotte were sitting at the table reading the paper and drinking coffee.

"We were wondering if you two were going to come out of the room today."

Eric smiled as he kissed his mother on the cheek. "I am sure the both of you were truly worried."

Keirra looked at the trio knowing there was a joke there somewhere, but she didn't get it. However, her cheeks did heat since Eric's parents seemed to be well aware of what they had been doing.

Now she knew what it felt like to be caught making out, although it had gone way beyond that. She looked up as Charlotte stood up from the table. Charlotte was smiling at both of them.

"Do you want me to make the two of you some breakfast?"

Eric shook his head as he held out a chair for Keirra. "No, Mom. I can handle it."

He looked at Keirra as she took her seat. "What would you like to eat?"

"Scrambled eggs and toast are fine," she murmured.

Eric nodded before walking over to the stove. Within minutes, he had the kitchen smelling good. A short while later, he set a steaming plate in front of her.

He joined her at the table, and they ate while conversing with his parents. By the time they finished eating, she was more than ready to get the trip to the precinct over. Eric grabbed their coats and led the way to his SUV. She was quiet during the ride to the precinct. She wanted to remain as calm as possible and take on Kayla's Zen-like mentality. It was difficult considering she was feeling sick to her stomach.

"What are you thinking about?"

Keirra shrugged. She really didn't know what she was thinking. There were too many thoughts flowing through her mind for her to focus on one. He didn't ask her any more questions, and she was grateful. Too many questions would only make her more nervous.

A short while later Eric pulled in front of the precinct. After taking a deep breath, she stepped out of the SUV. Eric took her hand and led her into the building. Somehow, she managed to put one foot in front of the other and walked into the police precinct. After they walked into the building, Eric led her straight to the front desk. The uniformed officer behind it smiled.

"Well hello, stranger. What brings you back to see us?"

Keirra watched Eric turn on his charm, and amazingly she wasn't jealous. The woman wasn't his type.

"Now you know I can't stay away from you too long."

Keirra shook her head, and a large plaque on the wall caught her attention. She let go of Eric's hand and walked toward the plaque. As she drew closer she saw that it was a memorial to all fallen officers. Her eyes automatically went in search of her father's name. When she found it, she smiled and touched the permanent etching. Seeing it didn't make her feel the dreaded sadness she thought it would. Her hand fell to her side as she began to remember all of the good times she had shared with her father.

"Is everything okay?"

Turning slowly, she smiled at Eric. It was one of true contentment. "Yes, it is."

And for the first time in her life since her father had passed, she truly felt like it would be.

Chapter Eighteen

"Where are you guys going?"

Keirra shrugged at Charlotte's question as she struggled to pull her hair up into a twist.

"I have no idea. Eric won't tell me."

Charlotte smiled. "My son has always been full of surprises. Sit down, dear, and I will help you."

"Yes, he is," Keirra murmured as she took a seat on the lid of the toilet. Charlotte pinned her hair up quickly and neatly. As crazy as it sounded, it was a reassuring act. She could remember her mother combing her hair as a little girl. It had been something that she liked, and it was a fond memory that she had of her mother.

Charlotte patted her shoulder. "I am finished. You look beautiful."

Charlotte gave her a kiss on the cheek. "Well you two have a wonderful time, and I will see you in the morning."

"We will, and thank you."

Charlotte left the bathroom, and Keirra put on a light touch of lip-gloss.

"You look beautiful."

She smiled as her gaze met his in the mirror. He was leaning against the doorway. The man was so sexy that she had to remember to breathe.

"Thank you. Let's see how long I can stay this way."

He laughed and held out his hand. "That will be an interesting challenge."

She shook her head. "I didn't mean for it to be."

Turning off the lights, she took his hand. "Okay, can you tell me where we are going now?"

He shook his head. "Not yet, but you will find out soon enough."

It was all she could do to not growl at him. She knew that it was a turn-on to him, and he didn't need any assistance in that area. They would never get out of the house if she did. He led her to the front door and helped her into her coat. After she was zipped up, he slid into his own jacket. He shocked her by not going out the front door. Instead, he led her down the hallway and through the kitchen. When he opened the back door, her eyes widened. There were candles lit all the way down the walkway. They went past the pool and down to the point where she couldn't see. Eric cut off the porch light, and she gasped. He didn't give her time to soak in the sight before leading her down the path. He led her to the massive camping tent that he had erected. He unzipped the front part, and she went inside with him stepping in behind her.

Her gaze swept the tent while he zipped the flap up. The tent had a romantic glow to it thanks to the battery-powered kerosene lamp. There were several blankets and a basket. Eric unzipped his coat and set it aside. Keirra did the same and was surprised the tent was as warm as it was. He indicated for her to have a seat, and she did so. Sitting down across from her, he reached for the basket. He pulled out a plate first then several containers of fruit. There seemed to be strawberries, watermelon, cantaloupe, and honeydew melon. He took out another container that held cheese and a container of crackers. He set the items aside, and then he pulled out two champagne flutes and a bottle of champagne

"This is very nice, Eric."

He smiled. "I am glad that you think so."

Eric reached for the container of fruit. She watched as he began to place food on the plate. By the time he finished he had a decent serving. He picked up a piece of cheese and offered it to her. She took it from him and closed her eyes as the cheese melted in her mouth. It was a cheese she hadn't tasted before. Her eyes opened, and he must have read the question in her eyes.

"Asiago."

He reached for the champagne and popped the cork. He poured a glass, before handing it to her and poured the other for himself. She took a sip and moaned in pleasure.

"This is very delicious."

He nodded, taking a sip from his own glass. The next few minutes were spent with them feeding each other. When she couldn't eat another bite, she held up her hands.

Eric cleaned up the mess and put the basket aside. He turned off the lamp. "Come lay by me."

She gave him an amused look. "Are we going to sleep out here?"

He chuckled. "No. We would probably freeze to death."

"I don't know. It is pretty warm right now," she murmured as she moved over to where he was.

He spread another blanket on the floor of the tent. She watched as he lowered onto the blankets before joining him. He grabbed two more blankets placing one under his head as a makeshift pillow. The other he pulled up over them. She snuggled up against him resting her head on his firm chest. Her mind was racing a mile a minute. Eric really was a good guy. Now she was starting to wonder if she was good enough for him. He seemed so perfect, and she was far from it.

"Why are you so interested in me?"

There was no hesitation is his answer. "Because you are sweet and caring. You are feisty and not afraid to give attitude. Because you are beautiful."

She was silent for a moment. He meant what he said. She could hear it in his voice. It was time she let him know what he was up against. Taking a deep breath she began telling him about the day that changed her opinion of officers of the law. She could still remember the day clearly.

Kristen, Kayla, and herself had been outside playing in the backyard. She would never forget their mother running to the back door frantically and rushing them into the house. She had piled them into the car and rushed them to the hospital. Kristen, Kayla, and she had sat in the backseat looking at each other in fear. They'd had no idea as to what had happened, but they had been scared. After arriving at the hospital, they had found out their father had been shot and had a very slim chance of making it. She remembered walking into the hospital and seeing her father's partner's distraught face.

There had been a few other officers there, and she could still picture the group separating as she, her sisters, and her mother walked down the hall. They had been taken to a room where her father had lain. He had told them all that he loved them and to be good for their mother. After that, he had been rushed off to surgery. If they could remove the bullet before it traveled, they might have been able to save him. It had been too late. Their father had died on the operating table.

She drew in a shaky breath and managed to smile even though she was certain Eric couldn't see it. "So now you see why I didn't want to take the risk with you."

He placed a reassuring kiss on her forehead. "Yes, I do, but I'm still glad you took the risk. I'm also glad you finally told me why you were so hesitant. I understand now."

She started to disagree with his statement but paused once she realized that he was right. She had already taken a risk and was too far in to go back. Now she just hoped that she wouldn't regret it.

* * * *

Keirra laughed as she struggled to get back into her clothing. After she told Eric the story about her father, he had slowly undressed her and made love to her until she couldn't think straight. They ended up falling asleep in the tent, and the rising sun had awakened them moments ago. There had been a little deception as to how warm it really was. Even though the two of them had been completely naked under the covers, their combined body heat had kept them warm. Now the both of them were shivering as they struggled to get into their clothes. They both managed to get dressed.

"I will put the tent up later," he forced out through chattering teeth.

She nodded as he helped her into her coat. Once he had his on, he unzipped the tent, and they ran for the house. When they made it inside, they were both breathless and laughing.

Charlotte was in the kitchen rummaging through the cabinets. She gave them a brief glance smiling once she did before turning back to the cabinet.

"Good morning, you two."

Eric walked over and gave his mother a kiss on the cheek. "Good morning, Mom. What are you looking for?"

She closed the cabinet. "Caffeine of any kind. I thought I had more than I did, but I'm out."

Keirra grinned. She and his mother had in common the need of caffeine the first thing in the morning. "Do you want me to go to the coffee store?"

"Yes, please."

He chuckled. "I will run to the room and get my keys."

Eric returned a moment later and looked at Keirra. "Would you like to come with me?"

Keirra hesitated. She really wanted to go upstairs and take a shower, but it wouldn't hurt to delay the shower a few minutes.

"Sure."

He led the way to his SUV.

"Get dark roast whole coffee bean. A one-pound bag if they have it," Charlotte called after them.

Eric nodded at his mother's last request as he opened the door for Keirra. Once she was in, he walked around to the driver's side and climbed in. After starting the engine, he backed out of the driveway and headed down the street. She leaned her head back against the headrest before looking over at him.

"When are we heading back to Baxley?"

She smiled knowing that she was ready to see her sisters. After last night, she was ready to get back because she felt as if they had come to a level in their relationship, and she wanted to see if things would be the same when they returned to Baxley. In some ways, it felt as if Atlanta had a lure over her, one that she was afraid would disappear when they returned.

"We will leave after breakfast, no later than noon if that is okay."

She nodded. No, she wasn't in a rush to get home because she was having a great time. She was just anxious to see her sisters and hear about their Thanksgiving. She had talked to them briefly, and from the noise in the background, they'd had as much fun as she did.

Thanksgiving dinner with the Brooks had been a lot of fun. The Brooks were a lot like her sisters and herself. They believed in having fun, and they had an immense amount of love for each other, even though that was the case. Dancing with Eric had probably been the most exciting thing. She would never forget that as long as she lived. Eric pulled into the parking lot of the coffee shop, and they walked inside.

"Is there anything else—"

"Well if someone had told me that we would be running into you today, I would have called them a liar."

Both Keirra and Eric looked in the direction that the comment came from. A smile came to Eric's face when he saw Tom and Jim. He informed her that they were two of the guys that he had served with at the Atlanta police department. He shook each of their hands.

"Hey, Jim. Tom."

Jim and Tom said their hellos, and Eric introduced Keirra as his girlfriend. She was able to keep a straight face this time. Hearing the word girlfriend still took a little getting used to.

Tom elbowed Jim. "Maybe it wasn't such a bad idea to move to Baxley."

Keirra felt herself flush with embarrassment at the compliment, and Eric shook his head as he put his arm around her waist. She leaned into his touch loving the feel of his strength his warmth.

"Well, I see that some things still haven't changed."

The three men talked for a few more minutes before Jim and Tom walked to their own table with their freshly brewed coffee in hand. Eric in turn went in search of the coffee bean that he knew his mother liked. He found it, and they headed for the checkout.

"Is there—"

Eric was interrupted as the door to the store was thrown open and a man came in shouting a woman's name. What was even scarier was that the man had a gun.

Eric moved quickly, actually dragging her behind a display for cover. His demonstration of agility and speed was something she would marvel at later. She could feel herself shaking with disbelief. Looking around she could see several people were taking cover under tables and whatever else they could get near. There hadn't been a lot of people in the shop at the time, twelve counting the four employees. The woman who the gunman was calling for came around the counter. He started ranting and raving about she couldn't leave him. The lady began trying to reason with him, and when that didn't work, Keirra could feel Eric shift behind her.

Looking over her shoulder, she saw him communicating with Tom and Jim and became nervous. She grabbed his arm when he went to move.

"What are you doing?"

He gave her an obvious look. "We have to help her."

She shook her head when she realized what Eric was getting ready to do. "Wait until the police get here."

He had the nerve to smile. "They are already here."

Her eyes widened when she grasped the meaning of his statement. "You need to wait for backup."

He nodded in the direction of Tom and Jim. "Over there."

Keirra shook her head. This didn't feel right at all, but she knew she wasn't going to convince him to sit still. She nodded and felt him move before pausing to give her a look.

"Everything will be okay. Just stay back, and stay low until you hear me telling you to come out."

He placed a brief kiss on her lips before moving away. Closing her eyes, she prayed for everyone's safety. She heard Eric's soothing voice, a voice that he had often used on her and had worked quite well, followed by Tom's. Now she hoped it had the same effect on the gunman. Both men seemed to be trying to convince the man he needed to put the gun down.

Her breath caught in her chest when she heard the gun go off. She heard Eric grunt right before the sound of a mad scuffle. When she gained the nerve to peak around the display, the sight before her brought her hand to her mouth in complete horror with a mix of relief. They had managed to subdue the gunman. Tom was lying with his full body weight on the man calling for one of the employees to come and help him while Jim had the woman the man had been after securely out of harm's way. She looked frantic, and Keirra couldn't blame her because she felt the same way. Eric was in the process of frantically trying to get his jacket off, and when he did, she saw why. He had been shot.

Her stomach dropped, and she rushed over to Eric while Tom called out to Jim for his handcuffs.

Jim looked at the woman he held. "Call 911."

The woman ran to the phone and did as she had been instructed. Her voice trembled as she tried to relay what happened, but Keirra barely heard her. Her focus was on Eric.

"Tell them we have an officer down."

The woman nodded at Jim's instruction. A towel appeared in her hands, and she placed it against Eric's shoulders, and he groaned. She flinched at the sound, and her hands began to shake, but she kept the pressure firm. She looked up and saw Jim helping Tom handcuff the gunman. She closed her eyes briefly then looked back down at Eric.

"What have you done?" she asked in a shaky voice.

He smiled at her. "I'm fine, Keirra. It isn't as bad as it looks."

She gave him a look of impatience and disbelief. "How would you know, Eric? You can't see the wound."

He brought his uninjured arm up and touched her cheek. The look in his eyes spoke of calmness, and he was cognizant, somewhat reassuring her. She kept the pressure on the wound and was handed another towel by someone else. Fortunately, he hadn't bled through the original towel, and he kept her distracted by talking to her, and after what seemed like an eternity, more uniformed officers and paramedics arrived. Keirra was forced to step back.

Her heart dropped to her stomach as they cut Eric's sweater away from the wound. It had been worse than she thought, but she only got a quick glance as the paramedics recovered the wound before loading him onto the stretcher.

"Tom, my cell phone, wallet, and keys are in the left pocket of my jacket. Drive Keirra to the hospital, and call my parents."

His calmness didn't do anything to reassure her this time. She had seen the wound and the blood that had oozed from it as soon as it was uncovered. It took a minute for the pressure of Tom's hand on her elbow to register. He led her to Eric's SUV and put her in on the passenger side. They followed behind the ambulance with Tom flipping opening Eric's cell phone and placing the call to Arthur and Charlotte. When they arrived at the hospital, Tom parked the car and rushed her to the emergency room, followed closely by Jim.

Tom was quick and efficient in getting the information needed. He led her to a chair where she could sit down, and she was glad because her knees were close to giving out. There were already officers at the hospital in response to the news of an officer being shot. It felt like she had traveled back in time as Tom led her through the crowd.

"Can I see the phone," she asked numbly. Tom gave it to her, and she tried to dial Kristen's number, but her hand was shaking so bad, and her vision was so blurry she couldn't manage it. Tom leaned down and gave her a comforting look before taking the phone out of her hand.

"Eric will be fine," he told her as he squeezed her hand, yet his touch did nothing to comfort her. The only thing that would set her mind at ease would be the sight of Eric walking out of the emergency room alive and unharmed.

"What number are you trying to dial?"

She stared at him blankly for a moment before realizing he was going to dial the number for her. She gave him Kristen's cell phone number, and he dialed it before handing the phone back to her. Her hands were a little sturdier, but her voice was still shaky. She got the voice mail and left a message. Hanging up, she went to hand it back to Tom, but he shook his head.

"You hold onto it in case they call back or if any of Eric's family call."

She nodded and set the phone in her lap before dropping her face into her hands. Her heart was racing. If Eric didn't make it, she didn't know what she was going to do. She was going to kill him if he did. One thing she knew for sure. After today was she couldn't be with Eric. Her heart and her blood pressure couldn't take the strain.

"Ms. Smith?"

Keirra looked up as a nurse approached with a gentle smile. Yet, her eyes held concern.

"Yes."

"We have to take Mr. Brooks up for surgery. The bullet is starting to travel, and we can lose him if we don't. He wanted me to come out here and tell you personally. I will be by his side the entire time, and I will keep you updated as much as possible and let you know when you can see him."

With that said, the nurse turned and rushed off. The shaking that Keirra had managed to get under control started again. She was going to lose him before she had the chance to tell him how she really felt. She dropped her face into her hands again, distraught that it seemed as if history was repeating itself. Was this how her mother had felt? Her mother had definitely been a lot calmer, but maybe it was because she had to be there for her children. There were no words to describe how she'd felt when her father had been rushed off to surgery.

She was starting to feel overwhelmed and needed to get some fresh air. Otherwise she was going to pass out. Never had she considered herself to be the fainting kind, but she was coming very close.

"Keirra."

Her head came up at the soft sound of Charlotte's voice. That is all it took to make her break. The tears came to her eyes followed by the first sob, and Charlotte sat down on the couch beside her and pulled Keirra into her arms.

"Everything will be okay. He is strong."

Keirra closed her eyes and prayed that Charlotte was right. Her heart truly couldn't take any more strain.

Chapter Nineteen

Keirra didn't know when she fell asleep, but somehow she had. Now someone was gently waking her. When she opened her eyes, she saw that it was Charlotte. She sat up abruptly when she remembered were she was. There was strain on everyone's face, and her stomach dropped.

"What is it? Is Eric okay?"

Charlotte smiled. "He is fine."

Keirra closed her eyes in relief. He was alive. Her eyes reopened when Charlotte spoke again.

"He is out of surgery, and they have moved him to his own room, so we can visit him. We thought you might want to see him first. He is still sedated for pain, so he may not be awake."

Keirra couldn't hide her surprise at their thoughtfulness, but agreed, especially after his sisters gave their nods of approval. After finding out what room he was in, she made the trip to his room. When she entered the room, the first thing she noticed were the machines he was hooked up to. The second was the large bandage that covered his shoulder. Tears sprang to her eyes as she walked closer to the edge of the bed. She touched Eric's hand, but he didn't respond. Fighting back a sob, she spoke.

"Oh, Eric, why did you have to try to play the hero?"

Even before she asked the question, she knew the answer. It was in his blood to protect and serve those who needed it. Knowing that he was still under the influence of drugs, she spoke from her heart.

"I love you, Eric, but I can't be with you. I wouldn't be able to take it if I lose you like I lost my father."

Keirra closed her eyes. She never thought she would hurt this much.

"I have to go now, and when I leave, I won't be back. I hope you can forgive me and move on. It is definitely for the best."

Keirra gave Eric one last look before leaning down to place a kiss on his lips, and by the time she reentered the waiting room, she was in tears again. She looked at Charlotte and Arthur.

"I have to go. I can't stay."

"Keirra."

She turned at the sound of her sisters calling her name. They rushed forward to embrace her, and she fell into their arms. The tears came again, and she clung to her sisters, not caring about anything else but having them with her now. Her sisters walked her over to a couch and sat down beside her. It took her several moments, but she managed to calm down a little and requested her sisters to take her home.

An hour later, they were on the road and heading back to Baxley. She sat in the back of Kristen's car next to Kayla while Kristen rode in the front and Randy drove. Most of the trip was in silence only interrupted by a few of her crying outbreaks. She felt awful that she was walking away from Eric when he needed her most, and her heart was breaking. But witnessing him being shot was enough to push her over the edge.

Leaning into her sister's warm embrace, she tried to believe walking away from Eric had been the right thing and hoped she could live with her decision. When they pulled up in front of the house she and Kayla shared, it was in the early morning hours, but it would still be several before the sun was up. Randy gathered up her suitcase while Kristen and Kayla escorted her up the walkway. They entered the house and led her to the couch.

"Now do you want to talk about it?"

She watched Randy make himself scarce, and she wanted to give him a hug for being so thoughtful, especially since he was going to be affected by this as well. With Eric being shot, it meant he would need to find a replacement for Eric until he came back.

"Keirra?"

She looked at Kristen and realized they were waiting on her to tell them what happened. Taking a deep breath, she tried to calm her nerves before she told her sisters about what had occurred that morning while having to pause at moments to keep from crying. By the time she finished, her sisters were just as upset as she was. Kristen was the one to speak first.

"I hope you and Eric can work this out."

Keirra shook her head. "I can't deal with this, Kristen. I refuse to jump every time the phone rings because I'm not sure if I am getting the call to tell me Eric has been injured again or worse yet dead."

Keirra stood up and walked to the opposite side of the room. "I can't take the stress."

She hugged herself as she emitted a humorless laugh. "I was shaking so bad I couldn't even dial your number. His former coworker had to dial it for me."

She turned to look at her sisters. "When I heard that gun go off and found out it was Eric that had been shot, I swear to you it was the worse feeling in the world."

Keirra paused. "Then to make it to the hospital and to find out that Eric was in danger of not making it. I can tell you I know exactly what Mom felt that day Daddy was shot."

Keirra closed her eyes, and different emotions raced through her. "I can understand why Mom was never the same afterward, and I don't want to live the rest of my life like that."

Kristen stood up and walked over to her sister. "Keirra, I can't tell you what choice to make. I can only tell you to think about it before you make a final decision."

Kristen embraced her tightly. "Take it from me when I say true love doesn't happen every day." She pulled back and looked at Keirra. "If you love Eric, go to him and tell him."

Keirra gave her sister a sad smile. "I already have."

She left out the part that Eric was unconscious and didn't hear her, but deep down, she knew she had made the right choice.

* * * *

Keirra sighed heavily as she turned off the water and stepped out of the shower. It had been three weeks since that horrible day in Atlanta, and she hadn't spoken to Eric since but knew through reports from other people, mainly his family, that Eric was doing okay. The memories of seeing him in the hospital bed after he had made it out of surgery were still fresh in her mind. Since she had come back home to Baxley, she had become a recluse, only dealing with people that she had to deal with and leaving the house when it was absolutely necessary. That basically meant work. She even refused to go to Sam's Café. All she wanted to do was sleep and be left alone. It was a sad thing to say because Christmas was next week, but she didn't feel merry at all.

Christmas was her favorite holiday, and she wasn't in the Christmas spirit at all. So far Kayla had done all of the Christmas decorations for the house by herself. Keirra was seriously considering seeing a psychologist. It felt as if she was losing her mind. Her every waking thought was of Eric. She had already lost her heart. Thankfully, her sisters had rallied around her.

They were supporting her as much as possible, not asking her questions or anything else of her. They knew that she had been pushed to her breaking point. She could also see the concern for her in their eyes, and she knew that she had to do something different. After toweling off, she slid into her bathrobe. She stepped into her room and stopped dead in her tracks and let out an ear-piercing scream.

Eric was sitting on her bed and didn't flinch at the sound. The way he looked, he was probably too out of it for the sound to even register. She brought a hand to her throat and tried to calm herself. This had been the last thing she'd expected.

She'd heard from Kristen he had come back into town two days ago. Randy and Kristen had gone over to check on him and had reported that he was doing okay. She hadn't expected to run into him so soon, especially not in her own bedroom. Was he even supposed to be out of bed? He looked worse than she had expected, but he still managed to look sexy as hell.

She met his eyes wearily. She wasn't ready for this confrontation. When he stood up, she unconsciously took a step back. He held out his hand, and without a reason as to why, she stepped forward and took it. Maybe it was because, deep down, she knew he wasn't going to hurt her. Or maybe it was because she was really delusional and losing her mind. Either way, it was too late to go back now.

She stopped in front of him, and he untied her rode. Turning slowly, he reached for the briefs that she had placed on the bed. He held them out, and she stepped into them. Eric dressed her and she closed her eyes in agony. Getting dressed had never been so erotic. She missed the feel of his hands. The bad thing was she was certain Eric didn't mean anything sexual by it.

His next action proved that. He stood and took her hand in his before leading her out of her room. He took her downstairs into the living room.

"We need to talk."

Her eyes closed, and she almost trembled at the sound of his voice. It had been so long since she had heard it.

"What would you like to talk about?" she whispered, glad that her voice was sturdier than she felt.

"Our future," he stated simply.

Her eyebrows rose. Leave it to Eric to get straight to the point and to have an ego while doing it. "Do we have a future?"

He gave her an irritated look. "Of course we do."

She closed her eyes and sighed. It was good to see him again. Three weeks ago, she had thought that possibility had been slim. Her eyes opened when he spoke again.

"Why did you leave me when I needed you?"

That statement brought her out of her trance. *Why did I leave him?* She sputtered, clenching her hands into fist.

"I must be out of my mind." She began to pace talking more to herself than to Eric. "He decides to go off and play hero, gets shot in the process, scaring me completely out of my mind, and he asks me why I didn't stay by his side when he needed me."

When she turned and faced him, she struggled to control her anger. "Maybe you coming here was a mistake." She nodded in the direction of the door. "You let yourself in, and you can let yourself out."

Turning, she headed for the kitchen. And to think that she had been worried out of her mind over such an egotistical idiot.

"Kayla let me in."

His response made her pause, but instead of replying she continued on into the kitchen. That would be taken up with Kayla, and she was going to kill her. Her older sister had picked up a nasty habit of meddling that was becoming irritating. She needed to do something to distract herself. Cooking would do it. Eric came into the kitchen just as she started to rummage through the refrigerator.

"Why do you fight what we could have?"

Her jaw almost dragged the ground. "You proved my worst fear true, and you have to ask? I told you how I lost my father, Eric, and I almost lost you the same way."

She slammed the door closed, and when she turned to face him, tears were in her eyes. "When we were in that coffee shop and I had that towel pressed to your shoulder, the only thing I could think was 'Please don't let him bleed to death on me. How will I explain this to his family if he does? How will I go on without him?'"

Her voice broke, and closing her eyes, she shook her head in anguish. "I thought you were my father happening all over again, and let me tell you, Eric, that was the worse feeling in the world. To sit there and wonder if those were the last moments I was going to spend with you and how would I go on if they were."

She barely managed to hold herself together as the emotions began to overwhelm her at the memory. "I don't want to have to sit at home or work and constantly think about if I am going to get the call that tells me you aren't going to come home to me."

Leaning against the counter she shook her head. She knew she couldn't do it. She had almost gone insane waiting for him in the waiting room of the hospital. Deep down, she knew she couldn't be with Eric. The worry would kill her.

"Can you guarantee me you won't run into another crazy person who decides to put another hole in you? Because, believe me, you have enough in you to last me a lifetime."

He shook his head. Stepping closer to her, he trapped her against the counter.

"No, I can't, but I can give you myself for as long as it lasts."

She shook her head. "That isn't good enough for me. I can't settle for that. I won't settle for that."

He gave her a quizzical glance. "Do you want me to give up the job?"

Keirra laughed. "No, because you can't, you won't. Being an officer is in your blood, like it was in my father's. Even if you don't have on the uniform, you are still a cop as you proved in Atlanta."

He leaned closer to her, and when he spoke, his voice was barely above a whisper. "Then what will be good enough? What will it take to convince you?"

Keirra smiled sadly at his pleading look and wanted to give in but knew she couldn't. "Unfortunately, I don't think anything will. You have a hero complex, Eric. You always have to come to the rescue. You always will, and as long as that is true, your regard for your own life will always come second."

She brought her hands up to put some space between them, trying to be careful of his injured shoulder. His proximity was making it hard for her to think, to be strong, but she had to be. This was one thing that she couldn't give in on.

"I just can't, Eric. You can't change, and there isn't anything you can do to convince me you can."

Eric shook his head. His expression told her that he didn't believe her. She knew Eric wouldn't give up easily, which was why she had been dreading this reunion. She had hoped she would have more time to prepare herself. It was hard to say no to him because she had let her guard down. She had let him into her life, her heart, but she had to say no. Cutting her ties to him was the only way she wouldn't have to worry about the constant fear of losing him. She couldn't take another chance on him.

"Would my love be enough?"

Her eyes widened briefly before she closed them. She immediately thought of him in the hospital bed recovering from his surgery. Keirra opened her eyes again, and he spoke softly.

"Do you love me?"

Her mouth opened, but no sound came out. Finally she nodded, knowing she had to be honest. Put it all out there so that there weren't any regrets. Nothing left unsaid.

"Yes, but—"

* * * *

Anything else she was going to say was cut off by his mouth because she had just told him she loved him, and that was all that mattered.

When he pulled back, there were tears in her eyes. He brought his hand up to her face.

"I can't promise you I won't be injured again, but I can promise you that I will do my best to remain safe and not always play the hero."

He placed another brief kiss on her lips. "With a woman like you waiting at home for me, I have a lot of motivation to stay alive and uninjured. I would have a lot of motivation to come home."

He wrapped his good arm around her as tightly as he could and breathed in her scent, a scent he had missed.

"How is your shoulder?"

He pulled back and smiled at her concern. Through accounts from his family, he knew his ordeal had been hard on Keirra. His mother reported that Keirra had cried most of the time. The rest of the time, she had spent in shock. He would do everything in his power not to do that to her again. The irony of the situation was he had only been injured while on duty once. The rest of his injuries had been obtained when he was just getting off duty or out of uniform. A fact he wouldn't bring up because it would only feed into her fears of his hero complex, something he would work on because he never wanted to scare Keirra as he had three weeks ago. It had been hard when he had awakened to find her not by his side. His entire family had torn into him for worrying all of them in such a fashion, but none more so than Keirra.

He had felt horrible knowing he had upset her so, especially since he knew what she had been through with her father. Hearing her tell that story had put clarity on the reason why she had avoided him in the beginning. Still, she had been willing to take the risk of giving him a chance. That was something he would never take for granted. Brushing her cheek with the back of his hand, he smiled.

"My shoulder is fine, but it would be a lot better if you could kiss it."

Keirra laughed at his suggestive statement. "Well then, we had better go upstairs and let you lie down. We wouldn't want to risk you falling and hurting yourself while I am checking on your wound."

Eric leaned forward until his mouth was near her ear. He whispered softly what risk he was willing to take, some of it in English and some in Spanish. The important thing was he told and showed her just how much he loved her.

* * * *

When Kayla came into the house half an hour later, her lips curled upward. Moans of passion reached her ears, and that was a good sign. Eric and her sister had made up a lot quicker than she had expected. She had honestly come back expecting to have to clean up wreckage, but Eric was more suited for her sister than she originally thought.

Stepping back outside the house, she closed the door. She would give the two an extra hour, maybe two. They had a lot of catching up to do, and who was she to get in the way? She had won the bet of who was going to fall in love next, but now it was inevitable that it was her turn. Now she just hoped her experience of falling in love would be as adventurous as it had been with Kristen and Keirra. She also knew that there would be hell to pay for everything she had put her sisters through, but if she ended up as content as her sisters were, it would be worth it.

About the Author

Stephanie Morris resides in Fort Worth, Texas. She has no children of her own, but has three nieces and one nephew and is proud to call Rocky, her three-year-old dog, her child. In her spare time, she enjoys reading, traveling, dancing, cooking, and spending time with her friends and family. She has been writing for several years now and has written several works in erotica and romance. This is her first published work, and she is looking forward to several more. She can be reached on MySpace at www.myspace.com/stephaniemorrisbooks or at www.stephaniemorris.webs.com.

Amira Press, LLC
www.amirapress.com

Her Every Fantasy
by Stephanie Morris

Kayla Smith is looking for a man that can satisfy her every need, and she has found him only he doesn't want the job. James Feldon has suffered through a messy marriage and has the scars to prove it. He isn't ready to become involved with another. Although he didn't realize how difficult that would be until Kayla became his teenage daughter's teacher. To make matters worse all four of his children have decided that they want a new mother, and they have chosen Kayla putting a completely different spin on his carefully laid out plan.